The Hidden War

Written By:

R.D. Wolfe

Table of Contents

Chapter I - Beneath the Surface

The air inside the mines was thick with dust, the scent of earth and sweat mingling into something that never quite left your lungs. The particles in the air clung to Cal's throat, turning each breath into a slow grind of grit against his teeth. His pickaxe struck stone with a dull *thunk*, the vibration rattling up his arms, swallowed instantly by the ceaseless clang of metal and the distant drone of machines gnawing at the earth. Automated drills and heavy loaders worked alongside human labor, extracting trexium at an industrial scale. Cal stood among the workers, hands wrapped tight around the worn handle of his tool. He wasn't a fighter. Not yet.

He was a digger, a miner, one of the many who pulled trexium from the earth. The lifeblood of the coalition, the resource that kept the machines running, the weapons charged, the walls standing. Without it, the coalition would collapse. Without it, they were no better than the scattered scavengers who fought over scraps in the wastelands beyond the valley.

Cal had been here since he was a child, raised in the mining camps by his parents, who had worked the tunnels before him. They were still alive, still digging, still struggling to provide for the family. His father's hands were worn and scarred from years of labor, his mother's cough a constant reminder of the dust that clung to their lungs. His father's voice echoed in his head—*Keep your head down, boy. It keeps you breathing.* But Cal's gaze drifted upward anyway, past the dark ceiling of the tunnels, toward where the world had to be waiting.

The foreman's voice cut through the cavern, barking orders as a new deposit was uncovered. The excitement rippled through the workers—Trexium veins meant bonuses, extra rations, a chance to move up in the ranks. Cal worked his pick harder, sweat dripping into his eyes. He had to get out of here. Not just out of the mines, but out of this life.

Cal's pick struck stone again, the vibrations numbing his fingers. He wiped sweat from his forehead, glancing toward the foreman's station. The older man stood near the entrance, arms crossed, watching him.

Not the crew. Just him.

Cal frowned, shifting his grip on his pick. The foreman's eyes lingered a moment longer before he turned, muttering something to another worker.

Joran nudged him. "What's with the staring contest?"

Cal shook his head. "No idea. He's been watching me like that all week."

Joran smirked. "Maybe you're working too hard. Making the rest of us look bad."

Cal huffed a small laugh, but something about the foreman's gaze stuck with him. He had felt it before. Like someone was paying attention to him when they shouldn't be.

A siren blared overhead. Cal froze, heart hammering. The siren's wail drilled into his skull, a rising, suffocating noise that stole the breath from his lungs. Somewhere in the darkness, a pickaxe clattered to the stone. Then another. Then the shouting began.

An attack.

Shouts erupted through the tunnels, workers scrambling for weapons—makeshift spears, repurposed mining tools. The mine had defenses, but nothing that could hold against a real incursion. There were also bunkers, but getting to them would mean cramming himself into rooms that barely had room for even the miners. The ground trembled beneath Cal's feet, dust raining from the ceiling. His fingers tightened around his pickaxe.

People ran, pushing toward the exits as the first explosion rocked the cavern. A dust cloud swallowed the tunnels, screams blending with the thunder of collapsing rock. Cal ducked, coughing, as figures pushed past him, their only thought to escape. He had a choice—follow them to the shelters below, or run for the surface.

His feet moved before his mind caught up, sprinting through the chaos, dodging falling debris and bodies scrambling for safety. The tunnels twisted upward, leading to the surface, where the Vanguard would be.

He burst through the mine's gates into the blinding light of day. The stronghold loomed ahead, its metal walls already lined with soldiers. And beyond that—

The Vanguard.

A blur of motion—then a roar of gunfire. The air cracked with the *whine* of charged rounds as the Vanguard descended. Cal barely saw them move. One second, the battlefield was chaos. The next, a wall of fire cut through the advancing horde. Cannons thundered from the front, tearing through bodies like paper. Above, Flyers dipped and wove, their sleek forms darting between collapsing structures. And somewhere, unseen until the moment of impact—Missiles fired in deadly arcs, each shot landing with pinpoint devastation.

In the midst of the battle, some wielded blades in close combat, their weapons cutting through flesh when the creatures got too close. Cal stood frozen, watching as the warriors he had only seen from afar now fought in the flesh. They were more than men. They were forces of nature.

Then he saw it—one of the undead, a former survivor and stronghold member, turned by the virus that plagued their daily existence against their own kind, breaking through the chaos, charging straight for him. His body refused to move. The thing was massive, its rotting limbs thicker than his torso, its hollow eyes locked onto him.

A blur of motion, and then steel cut through flesh. A Vanguard warrior landed between Cal and the beast, driving a blade through its skull. The creature crumpled, lifeless, before Cal even had time to react.

"What the hell are you doing up here?" a voice snapped. He barely had time to turn before hands grabbed him, yanking him backward.

His friend, Joran, pulled him toward the entrance to the tunnels, shoving him toward the shelters. "You always do this, Cal. You're going to get yourself killed one day."

Cal barely resisted, his eyes lingering on the Vanguard as they fought. As Joran dragged him down, the last thing he saw was the warrior who had saved him, already turning back into the fray, never sparing him another glance.

To them, he was another worker, another miner. But standing there, watching the Vanguard fight, he felt something shift inside him. He had seen their strength, their discipline—and something about it called to him.

The battle was over. The stronghold had survived—this time. Fires still burned along the barricades, and the scent of blood and smoke clung to the air. The dead were being gathered, the wounded tended to, but for most, the night was over.

Cal and Joran sat near the shelter entrance, watching the cleanup. Joran exhaled sharply, running a hand through his sweat-matted hair. "You're an idiot, you know that?" he muttered. "One of these days, you're not going to be lucky."

Cal stayed quiet, his gaze fixed on the battlefield beyond the walls. "I had to see them."

"You've seen them before," Joran shot back. "But this time, you almost got ripped apart. What were you thinking?"

Cal hesitated before answering. "That I don't belong down here."

Joran scoffed, shaking his head. "You belong where you stay alive. Where your family needs you. The Vanguard aren't for people like us, Cal. We dig. We survive. That's our job."

Cal clenched his fists, the memory of the Vanguard warrior's blade flashing through his mind. "Maybe I want more than just surviving."

Joran sighed, rubbing his temples. "Then you're going to have to find a way that doesn't get you killed. Listen, I know you stay up at night reading and studying all those books and data pads, and god knows you go through them like no one I've ever met, I don't know how you do it honestly, but that's besides the point. You're losing yourself in ambition, man. You're missing what's right in front of you."

Cal exhaled, letting the thought settle. Maybe Joran was right. Maybe the mines were the only place for people like them. But as he looked out at the Vanguard standing watch under the smoldering sky, he knew one thing—he wasn't ready to accept that just yet.

Chapter 2 - A Step Too Far

The morning after the attack, the mines were different. No shouting. No banter. Just the quiet scrape of pickaxes, the occasional clink of metal against stone. Even the air felt wrong— still heavy with the stench of burned flesh and scorched rock.

"They almost got through last night," a voice murmured nearby.

"Too close," another answered. "Did you see the ones they dragged out?"

The pickaxes didn't swing as hard. Nobody wanted to make too much noise, as if the creatures would hear and come back.

The battle had left scars—not just on the walls, but on the people. Some workers had died. Others had been injured. The foreman barked orders, trying to reestablish routine, but there was a weight in the air that hadn't been there before.

The stronghold pulsed with movement, every path crammed with soldiers and workers. Supply carriers wove through the narrow walkways, barking at slower men to clear a path. The air shifted the deeper Cal went—less dust, more the thick, greasy scent of cooked rations and burning fuel.

Outside the barracks, a few off-duty soldiers slumped on overturned crates, dealing out a battered deck of cards. One of them, a wiry man with a fresh bandage wrapped around his arm, let out a dry chuckle at his hand. "Lucky draw," he muttered, tossing down a pair of matching cards.

Another soldier scoffed, leaning back against a supply crate. "Luck's got nothing to do with it, Ferris. You cheat every damn time."

The laughter that followed was short, cut off too soon—more reflex than joy. Even at rest, their eyes flicked toward the perimeter, their hands never far from their weapons.

Cal paused outside a mess hall where workers gathered for their evening rations. The line moved slowly, bowls of thick stew ladled out with precise, measured portions. He considered joining them, but decided against it. The night air called to him, the idea of being trapped in the same cycle of work and rest suffocating.

As he moved further from the barracks and the scent of rations and oil faded, the stronghold grew quieter. The sounds of conversation and clinking metal gave way to the steady hum of machinery deeper in the tunnels. His steps slowed as he approached the familiar corridor leading to his family's quarters, the air thick with the ever-present dust of the mines. Only then did he allow himself to relax, if only slightly. The small, dimly lit room was home—if the word even applied to a space carved from rock and metal. His father sat at the table sharpening a worn-down pickaxe, while his mother stirred a pot over a crude stove, her cough punctuating the silence.

"You're late," his father muttered without looking up. "Foreman giving you extra work?"

"No," Cal said, rubbing the back of his neck. "I just needed some air."

His mother gave him a sharp glance. "You went to watch them again, didn't you?"

Cal hesitated. Lying was pointless. "Yeah."

His father exhaled slowly, rubbing his hands over his face before setting the pickaxe aside. He didn't look at Cal right away, just stared at the ground, his fingers idly tracing the deep calluses along his palm. "You're not one of them, Cal," he said finally. "You know that, right?"

Cal swallowed, his throat dry. "I know." But the words felt like someone else had said them.

His mother sighed through her nose, resting a hand against the table. Her fingers tapped against the wood—slow, thoughtful. "It's not that we don't understand, Cal," she murmured. "It's just..." She shook her head, looking at him like she was already mourning who he wanted to become. "Not that easy."

Cal clenched his fists. "Maybe I don't want it to be."

His father sighed again, rubbing his forehead. "It doesn't matter what you want. We survive. That's what matters."

Cal didn't argue. There was no point. But deep down, he wasn't ready to accept that just yet.

Later that evening, Cal and Joran slipped away from their quarters. The stronghold was vast, with more than just mining tunnels. There were armories, barracks, supply depots—places workers weren't meant to wander. But tonight, curiosity overruled caution.

They moved through the dim corridors, keeping to the shadows when guards passed.

"You sure about this?" Joran whispered, glancing behind them.

"If we're stuck living here, might as well learn more about it," Cal murmured back.

Joran sighed. "Yeah, but how do you know where to go?"

Cal hesitated. "The guards rotate every fifteen minutes. They take the same route every time—three down the barracks hall, two through supply, one up top watching the east gate. We've got a four-minute window between shifts."

Joran blinked. "And you just... noticed that?"

"Yeah."

"Damn." Joran shook his head. "You ever think about putting that brain to use for something other than getting us both killed?"

"Yeah," Cal sighed. "All the time. You?"

Joran huffed. "Not really. I prefer staying out of trouble."

They crept past an administrative office, its doors slightly ajar. Inside, a commanding officer sat at a desk, speaking to a subordinate. Maps were sprawled across the surface, marked with supply routes, patrol patterns, and key stronghold locations. Cal stopped, peering in, intrigued.

"Come on," Joran hissed, tugging his sleeve. "If they catch us here—"

But Cal wasn't listening. His eyes landed on an insignia on the officer's uniform—one different from the standard soldiers. This wasn't a Vanguard, but someone who had authority, someone who helped organize the coalition's operations. It was a rare look at how decisions were made, how power moved through the coalition beyond the mines, farms, and battlefields.

Footsteps echoed down the hall. The boys ducked back into a shadowed alcove as two soldiers passed, talking in hushed voices. Cal exhaled slowly, adrenaline surging through him.

"This is a bad idea," Joran muttered.

"Then go back," Cal said, moving ahead.

Joran cursed but followed.

They hesitated at a junction, unsure of which way to go. Just then, two soldiers passed them, deep in conversation.

"Training's wrapping up soon. The recruits are getting torn apart by the Commander today," one of them muttered.

"Good. We need better fighters. Last run barely held the line."

Cal caught Joran's eye, then subtly nodded toward the direction the soldiers had come from. Joran exhaled through his nose, clearly irritated, but followed as Cal took the lead.

They moved cautiously, keeping a few paces behind another pair of soldiers heading the same way. As they turned a corner, the air shifted. The scent of sweat and oil thickened, and the sound of boots striking the floor in perfect rhythm echoed down the hallway.

They had found it. The training hall. The place smelled of sweat and oil; the walls lined with racks of firearms and melee weapons alike. But instead of a large group of Vanguard, as Cal had expected, there was only one. A single Vanguard warrior, standing with a group of soldiers. The man exuded authority, his posture rigid, his armor heavier than the others. The soldiers seemed to be listening intently as he issued orders.

Cal and Joran tried to slip past unnoticed, but the Vanguard's gaze flicked toward them immediately. "Stop."

The soldiers turned, hands resting on their weapons.

Joran stiffened. "Great."

The Vanguard studied them, his presence alone enough to command respect. "What are you two doing here?"

Cal hesitated. "We were just—"

"Looking?" the Vanguard cut in. "Workers aren't allowed in this section. You know that."

"I wanted to see," Cal said, his voice steadier than he felt. "What it takes to be one of you."

The Vanguard didn't answer right away. He just looked at Cal, like he was weighing something unseen. The silence stretched, the tension thick enough to choke on. Then, with a small shake of his head, he turned to one of the soldiers.

"Take them to Varek." A pause. Then, almost as an afterthought—"Let's see if he finds them useful."

Joran groaned. "We are so dead."

They were escorted through the stronghold, past storage areas and briefing rooms, before stopping at a heavily guarded office. The soldier knocked once before stepping aside. "Sir, two miners were found where they shouldn't be."

A voice from within replied, "Send them in."

Cal and Joran stepped inside. A man sat behind a metal desk, his uniform crisp, his expression unreadable. He wasn't a Vanguard, but he outranked everyone they had encountered so far.

Commander Varek leaned forward, fingers steepled. "You two have an interesting way of spending your free time. Care to explain?"

Cal met his gaze and, for once, didn't back down. "I want to be something more than a miner."

Varek studied him before a small, knowing smirk touched his lips. "Then you should've found a better way to start."

Cal didn't flinch. Whatever happened next, he knew one thing—he wasn't invisible anymore.

Chapter 3 - Orders and Opportunities

Cal sat stiffly in the metal chair across from Commander Varek, his palms pressed against his knees to keep from fidgeting. Joran sat beside him, arms crossed, doing his best to look disinterested, though the occasional nervous bounce of his foot gave him away.

Varek's gaze flicked between them, unreadable, the silence stretching long enough that Cal felt every second press down on his chest. The air in the room was still, thick with something unspoken. Finally, Varek exhaled sharply, drumming his fingers once against the metal table before leaning back.

"Miners sneaking into military zones," he mused. "Not exactly something we tend to ignore." His voice was even, almost bored, but there was an edge beneath it, a weight that made the words heavier.

Cal kept his expression neutral, but beside him, Joran let out a nervous chuckle that didn't quite reach his eyes. "If we knew how much trouble, we'd have run the other way."

Varek's brow lifted slightly. "And yet here you are."

The room was sparse, more functional than decorative. A single dim light overhead flickered slightly, casting long shadows on the stone walls. A thick map of the region lay sprawled across the desk between them, covered in faded lines and inked notations. Cal's eyes flickered over it, catching glimpses of locations he'd only ever heard about in passing. Supply routes. Fortifications. Strategic points outside the stronghold.

He forced himself to focus back on Varek before the commander could catch him staring.

"I should send you both back to the mines," Varek said, his tone casual, as if the decision had already been made. "Punishment detail. Hard labor. That's the easy call."

He leaned forward slightly, his gaze locking onto Cal's. "But before I do, humor me—what were you hoping to find?"

Cal's throat felt tight. His fingers curled against his knees, nails pressing into fabric. "I..." He swallowed, forcing himself to hold Varek's stare. "I wanted to see how they train. How they become Vanguard." The words felt too small, too simple for everything he had been thinking.

Varek tilted his head, studying him like a puzzle he wasn't sure was worth solving. "And you thought watching from the shadows was the way to do it?"

Cal's jaw tensed, his fingers curling into fists in his lap before he forced them open. He exhaled sharply through his nose, staring down at the map sprawled across the desk as if the answers might be hidden in the ink. When he spoke, his voice was quieter at first, almost uncertain. "No..." He hesitated, then looked up, determination overtaking hesitation. "But I don't want to be a miner for the rest of my life. I want to know what it takes to be something more."

Joran let out a quiet sigh, shaking his head. "Here we go..."

Varek tapped his fingers against the desk. "You're not the first miner to say that, and you won't be the last."

"Even the regular soldiers go through years of training. The Vanguard? They don't pick recruits on a whim. They don't have the numbers to waste on people who can't make the cut."

Cal hesitated, his fingers tapping anxiously against his knee. The weight of the room, of Varek's stare, pressed down on him. His chest tightened as the words fought their way up his throat. If he didn't say it now, he never would. He gritted his teeth, inhaled sharply, and finally leaned forward, his voice edged with urgency. "Then tell me how to start." His hands curled into fists. "What does it take to even have a chance?"

Varek let the silence stretch between them. Then, finally, he smirked, but there was no warmth in it. "It takes more than sneaking around in places you don't belong."

He stood, plucking a sheet of paper from his desk with deliberate ease. "A week of extra shifts. On top of your usual mining work. You'll report to the supply depot before first light." He let the silence hang for a beat. Then—"Late? You double the time."

His smirk faded. "Consider it your first lesson in discipline."

Joran groaned. "You've got to be kidding me."

"You're getting off easy," Varek replied flatly. "But if you actually want to learn something useful, pay attention while you're there. The supply depot handles logistics, weapons distribution, and troop movements. You might find some answers in there—if you're smart enough to recognize them."

Cal's heart pounded, but he kept his expression neutral. "Understood, sir."

Cal stood, ready to leave, but Varek wasn't dismissing him yet.

The commander leaned back slightly, tapping his fingers against the desk in thought. "You're not the first miner to want out. You won't be the last. But someone's taken an interest in you."

Cal blinked. "What?"

Varek tilted his head slightly, studying him like a puzzle he hadn't quite solved. "Your foreman flagged you in his reports— said you weren't like the others. Smarter. Quicker. Most workers don't go looking for more responsibility." He exhaled through his nose. "And now, here you are, putting yourself exactly where people like me can see you."

Cal's mouth felt dry. "I just—"

"Don't care," Varek cut him off. "Keep showing up in places you shouldn't be, and someone will decide where you belong. And it won't be in the mines."

There was something about the way he said it—not a threat, not a warning. Just a fact.

Cal hesitated before nodding. "Understood."

"Good." Varek waved a dismissive hand. "Get out of my office."

The next morning came too soon. After spending most of the night staring at the ceiling, replaying every word of his conversation with Varek, Cal forced himself out of bed before the first shift bell rang. The exhaustion clung to him, but he pushed it aside as he made his way to the mines for another grueling day of work. Cal's arms ached as he forced himself through another grueling shift in the mines, each swing of his pickaxe heavier than the last. The tunnels buzzed with quiet conversation, the previous night's events still fresh in his mind, but no one had time to dwell on anything beyond their work quotas. By the time his shift ended, sweat clung to his skin, and his fingers were raw from gripping his tools.

After finishing their morning shift in the mines, Cal barely had time to eat before making his way to the supply depot for the punishment detail that afternoon. The exhaustion sat deep in his muscles, but he pushed forward. As he stepped into the dimly lit corridors, the ever-present hum of machinery filling the air, he spotted Joran waiting near a junction, rubbing the sleep from his eyes.

"You look terrible," Joran muttered, falling into step beside him.

"Didn't sleep much," Cal admitted. "Kept thinking about what Varek said."

Joran let out a half-hearted chuckle. "You're thinking too much about this. We're just moving crates, not getting inducted into the Vanguard."

Cal exhaled sharply but didn't respond. Varek's words echoed in his mind: *You might find some answers in there—if you're smart enough to recognize them.* He had no idea what that meant yet, but he wasn't about to waste the chance. His mind was already working through what he might learn today, what small pieces of information he could gather. The weight of their punishment hung heavy between them, but for Cal, it wasn't just about punishment—it was an opportunity.

By the time they arrived at the depot, exhaustion had already set in from the days work. The air was thick with the scent of oil, dust, and metal, a stark contrast to the damp, earthy confines of the mines. Cal rolled his shoulders, willing the stiffness from his muscles, knowing that another long shift was just beginning. The supply depot sprawled ahead of them, an intricate maze of storage crates, weapon racks, and workers hauling supplies between stations with the efficiency of a well-oiled machine. The rhythmic clatter of crates being stacked formed a steady undercurrent of noise, broken only by the occasional barked order from the quartermasters overseeing the chaos.

Cal barely had time to take it all in before a rough voice cut through the din. "You two! Over here!"

They turned to find themselves under the scrutiny of a grizzled quartermaster built more like a boulder than a person. His eyes, sharp and unyielding, sized them up in an instant, and whatever assessment he made was clear in the unimpressed curl of his lip. One of the nearby workers muttered, "Rusk's gonna eat 'em alive."

"You two? You're on inventory duty," Rusk barked. "You log every crate that comes through here, where it's going, and who signed off on it. If anything's out of order, you report it to me. You screw up, you do it again until you get it right."

Joran let out a breath. "I thought we were in trouble, not doing paperwork."

Rusk scowled. "You think logistics isn't important? You think the Vanguard just get their weapons handed to them without this place running like a machine? Every round of ammunition, every ration pack, every armor plate, and every ounce of trexium has to be accounted for. That mineral keeps everything running—from our defenses to the very weapons they use. Lose track of it, and you might as well hand the enemy the key to the gates. Now shut up and get to work."

Rusk didn't seem like a man to trifle with, so they shut up and got to work.

Cal ran his finger down the ledger, eyes scanning the neatly inked lists of inventory. His hands were raw from mining all morning, but now, standing over the records desk, he could focus.

A soldier strolled past, mid-conversation with another. "They're pulling Vanguard out of the western patrols. Heard command's reallocating gear."

"About time," the other muttered. "You see the latest requisitions? They get armor upgrades while we're stuck patching old plates with scrap."

Cal barely listened. His attention was on the numbers. The Vanguard shipments weren't just prioritized—they were separate. Special orders. Custom-fitted armor, enhanced rations, weapons that weren't even listed for standard troops. Not just soldiers. A different class entirely.

His fingers drummed against the ledger, the pattern clicking into place.

"You're staring at those numbers like they're going to tell you a secret," Joran muttered, stacking a pile of manifests beside him. "What's on your mind?"

Cal tapped a finger against a list of requisition orders. "The Vanguard operate differently than the soldiers. They get priority equipment, separate meal rations, and their deployment orders aren't listed alongside the standard forces."

Joran frowned. "Yeah, because they're the elite. Everyone knows that."

"But it's not just that. Look at this." Cal pointed at a document with several marked-out locations. "Their deployment sites aren't static. They move constantly, never staying in one place too long. And these supply requests—they're tailored. Someone plans their gear based on what they're up against."

Joran leaned in, following the notations. "So? You got some kind of big plan, or are you just staring at numbers, hoping they make sense?"

Cal thought for a moment. "It tells me that if I want to understand how they fight, I need to know who's making those decisions. Someone up the chain determines where they go, how they're equipped, and what missions they take. That's the person I need to learn from."

Joran exhaled, rubbing his temples. "I can already feel the trouble you're going to get us into."

Before Cal could respond, a voice cut through the depot.

"Rusk! Where the hell is that requisition order for the northern perimeter?"

A soldier stormed in, frustration evident. He wasn't a Vanguard, but he carried himself like someone who commanded respect.

Rusk grumbled, flipping through a stack of papers. "It's here somewhere, Lieutenant. Maybe if half the paperwork I get wasn't smudged with dirt and sweat, I'd find it faster."

The soldier scowled, but his gaze flickered to Cal and Joran. "Who are they?"

"Punishment detail," Rusk said without looking up. "Caught sneaking where they shouldn't be. Figured they could use some time learning how an army actually functions."

The soldier snorted. "Good. Maybe they'll learn something useful."

Cal met his gaze. "Or maybe we'll learn how things really work."

The lieutenant's smirk faltered for a fraction of a second before he grabbed his requisition form and left.

Joran leaned over. "See? That right there? That's the kind of talking that's going to get us reassigned to shoveling latrines."

Cal wasn't so sure. Something about the way the lieutenant hesitated told him he was on the right track.

He wasn't just moving supplies.

He was learning how to move up.

Chapter 4 – A Different Breed

The first few days blurred together—lifting, logging, moving, lifting again. The same routines, the same sore muscles. At first, it felt like the mines. Dig, haul, repeat. But here, the weight wasn't just in the crates. It was in the numbers. The patterns.

"Vanguard requisition list," a quartermaster barked, shoving a clipboard into Cal's hands. He took it without thinking, scanning the entries.

Armor plating, reinforced. Ammunition, specialized. Rations—twice the portion of standard soldiers. Trexium, more than enough to fight off a hundred infected.

Not just better equipment. Priority equipment. Custom orders. While standard forces patched old gear, the Vanguard had shipments marked confidential.

"That list isn't for you, miner," Rusk, the supply officer, snapped, snatching it back. "Move."

Cal did as he was told, but the numbers stuck. They weren't just fighting differently. They were being prepared differently.

Joran, however, treated it as just another punishment. "I swear, if I never see another stack of manifests again, it'll be too soon," he muttered as they worked late into the evening. "I don't know what you think you're learning from this, but it's still just moving crates."

Cal didn't argue, but he knew better. It wasn't just crates. It was everything. Every crate had a purpose, every number on the manifest meant something. He just had to figure out what.

One evening, near the end of their punishment detail, Cal found it.

A small discrepancy in the supply records.

He frowned at the requisition order in his hands. "Joran, look at this."

"If it's not food, I don't care." Joran stretched, cracking his back. "Unless you found where they stash the real rations, in which case, I absolutely care."

Cal shoved the ledger toward him. "Trexium shipment. Supposed to go to the western perimeter. Never logged as received. No return slip. No redistribution. Just gone."

Joran frowned, tracing a finger over the entry. "Could be an error."

"It's not one crate," Cal said, voice low. "It's the whole shipment."

Joran exhaled through his nose. "So... someone's skimming? Or something bigger?"

"I don't know." Cal clenched his jaw. "But if it's just a mistake, why scrub the records?"

Joran frowned but shrugged. "So, tell Rusk and let him yell at someone about it."

Cal hesitated. He could do that. He could hand it off and walk away. But something about it nagged at him. He had spent the past week memorizing these patterns, understanding how supplies moved. And this? This wasn't normal.

He wasn't taking it to Rusk, he was taking it to Varek.

Commander Varek sat behind his desk as Cal placed the requisition report in front of him. Varek didn't look up right away. The scratch of his pen filled the silence, the slow, deliberate strokes of a man who wasn't in a hurry. Only when he was finished did he set it aside, fingers lacing together as he regarded Cal.

"This had better be worth my time, Miner."

The paper in Cal's grip crinkled slightly. He steadied his breath. "There's a problem with the supply logs. A shipment of trexium—meant for the western perimeter—never arrived. No redistribution records. No return slip. Just disappeared."

Varek finally took the page, his eyes flicking over the numbers with a practiced efficiency. He didn't react, didn't even arch a brow. The silence stretched, thick and heavy.

"You're sure about this?"

"I triple-checked."

Another beat of quiet. Then, slowly, Varek folded the paper, tucking it inside his coat. "Either someone's stealing, or someone's covering something up." His voice was even, but something unreadable flickered beneath it.

He met Cal's gaze. "And in either case, that's a problem."

Then, without a word, he stood, the chair scraping against the stone floor, and walked slowly to the door. The click of the lock sounded louder than it should have in the tight space, making Cal's pulse jump. His fingers twitched at his sides, a sudden awareness creeping into his limbs—was locking the door a formality? Or a warning?

Cal tensed.

Varek turned back, folding his arms as he leaned against the desk, his gaze unreadable. "You're sure about this, Miner?" The air in the room felt heavier, charged with something unspoken. "You're sure about this? You didn't just get numbers mixed up? Didn't overhear something and think you were onto a grand conspiracy?"

Cal felt his mouth go dry, but he refused to back down. "I triple-checked," he said, his voice steady despite the nervous energy twisting in his stomach.

Varek exhaled, rubbing a hand over his chin. He let the moment drag, eyes never leaving Cal's, as if waiting for him to reconsider. "You know what trexium is used for, Miner?" When Cal didn't waver, he finally spoke again. "You know what trexium is used for, right?"

"Powering everything?"

"More than that." Varek tapped the paper. "This much trexium going missing isn't just an oversight. Either someone's stealing it, or someone's covering something up. And in either case, that's a problem."

Cal swallowed hard, shifting his weight from foot to foot. He wasn't sure what answer he wanted. "What are you going to do?"

"That's not your concern, Miner." Varek folded the paper with slow precision, tucking it into his coat as he leveled Cal with a look that sent a chill down his spine. "But I'll tell you this—"You found something useful," Varek murmured, almost amused. "That makes you useful." He leaned back slightly, studying Cal with something close to interest. "And being useful? That means people will watch you."

Cal swallowed.

"Tomorrow," Varek continued, "you're done at the supply depot. I want you at the training yards. Not training. Observing."

The words weren't an offer. They weren't a punishment. They were something else. A door being opened—or a cage being built.

Cal's fingers curled into fists. He exhaled. "Understood."

The door clicked shut behind him, sealing Varek's office—and whatever Cal had just stepped into—firmly behind him. His breath came slow, measured, but his pulse betrayed him, hammering in his ears. Opportunity or trap, it didn't matter. He was already in.

The next day, after finishing his shift in the mines and grabbing a quick meal, Cal made his way toward the mess hall courtyard, where workers and soldiers alike gathered in small clusters. The space was filled with the low hum of conversation, the scrape of metal trays against stone tables, and the occasional bark of orders from passing officers.

In the far corner, away from the main crowd, Joran sat alone on a wooden bench beneath a rusted overhang, absently stirring his food with his spoon. When Cal sat down beside him, Joran didn't look up.

"Varek pulled you in, didn't he?" Joran finally asked.

Cal hesitated, then nodded. "I'm just watching."

"Yeah. For now."

Cal sat beside him, stretching out his sore legs, letting the silence settle between them. The tension in Joran's posture was obvious—the way his shoulders hunched slightly forward, the way he kept his eyes fixed on his tray, as if avoiding the conversation they both knew was coming. The weight of unspoken words thickened the air between them, pressing down like the heat before a storm. Joran exhaled heavily, rubbing a hand over his face before setting his spoon down with a soft clink against his tray. He finally turned his gaze to Cal, his usual dry amusement absent from his expression.

"I just don't want to lose you, man." His voice was quieter now, less sharp, and edged with something that almost sounded like fear. "I get it—you want out of the mines. Hell, we all do. But this? This is different. You keep pushing this, and one day you're not gonna walk back through those gates."

Cal shifted uncomfortably. "It's not like that, Joran."

Joran scoffed. "You think Varek is just letting you watch because he likes your curiosity? No, Cal. He's pulling you in. That's how it starts. First, you're just observing, then maybe you're running messages, then before you know it, you're holding a rifle, and then—" Joran stopped himself, shaking his head. "I don't want to see you go out there just to end up as another name on a list."

Cal clenched his fists beneath the table, frustration and guilt twisting inside him. "You think I haven't thought about that? You think I don't know the risks?" He exhaled sharply, forcing himself to calm down. "But I can't just keep my head down forever. I can't live my whole life swinging a pickaxe, waiting for the next attack to kill us all, anyway. At least this way, I have a choice."

Joran watched him closely, searching his face for something— doubt, hesitation, a reason to believe Cal wasn't serious about all of this. When he found nothing but quiet determination, he let out a slow, tired chuckle, the sound lacking its usual bite. "Damn it, Cal. You've always been stubborn."

Cal smirked, but it didn't quite reach his eyes. "Yeah, well, so have you."

Joran sighed again, his fingers drumming lightly on the edge of his tray. Then, as if making peace with whatever battle was playing out in his head, he reached across the table and punched Cal lightly on the arm. "Fine. But if you get yourself killed, I swear I'll find a way to be pissed at you from the afterlife."

Cal laughed, tension easing between them. "Deal."

Joran shook his head, a reluctant grin tugging at his lips. "Alright, go watch your soldiers. But if they put you on latrine duty, I get to say I told you so."

"You coming?" Cal finally asked.

Joran sighed and shook his head. "Nah. I think I've had enough punishment for one lifetime."

Cal wanted to argue, to tell him it wasn't about punishment. But he didn't. Joran wasn't wrong. They were stepping onto different paths.

"I'll see you later, then," Cal said.

Joran smirked. "Yeah. Try not to get yourself shot."

The training yards were unlike anything Cal had ever seen up close. Soldiers sparred with live weapons, drilled in formations, and trained with a level of precision that miners could never hope to match. And the Vanguard—when they moved, it was like watching something beyond human. Efficient, deadly, and terrifyingly controlled.

Cal stood at the edge, arms crossed, trying to blend into the background as the training unfolded before him. He wasn't alone, though. A soldier had been stationed near him, looking dour and unhappy.

"Don't do anything stupid, Miner," the soldier muttered without looking at him. "I don't feel like explaining to Varek why you got flattened."

The midday heat settled over the training yard, sweat beading on the backs of soldiers as they moved through their drills. The smell of dust and gunpowder clung to the air, mixing with the acrid tang of oil from the weapons racks. He noticed how some soldiers adjusted their grips, how their stances shifted with fatigue—details he never would have considered before...

A group of standard soldiers loitered near the weapon racks, wiping sweat from their brows and refitting their gear. Some of them cast amused glances in Cal's direction.

"Hey, Revik, they got you babysitting now?" one of them called out, smirking.

The soldier beside Cal—Revik, apparently—sighed. "Just making sure the miner doesn't get himself killed. Varek wants him watching."

"Guess we're scraping the bottom of the barrel for recruits now," another soldier muttered, shaking his head as he wiped sweat from his brow. Their training session had just wrapped up, and most of them were either catching their breath or swapping gear. He shot Cal a glance before adding, "Hope you brought a shovel, miner."

A few others snickered. "Maybe he's here to teach us how to dig trenches."

"Might be useful," another soldier cut in, stretching out his sore arms. "You lot probably don't even think about where half the supplies come from. You just take what's handed to you. Let me guess—how long does it take to extract a full trexium vein?"

The first soldier scoffed. "A day? Two if it's deep?"

Cal shook his head. "Try weeks. And that's if the vein is stable. Sometimes we dig for months just to get a fraction of what you burn through in a single battle. The deeper the vein, the harder it is to reach, and sometimes it collapses before we can even extract half of it. Every chunk of trexium that powers your fancy armor and rifles? That costs blood, sweat, and broken backs to pull from the ground."

Cal clenched his jaw, exhaling slowly through his nose to keep his temper in check. He could feel the scrutiny of the soldiers around him, the weight of their unspoken judgment. Revik chuckled beside him, shaking his head slightly.

He could already hear Joran in his head, warning him not to pick a fight, not to let them bait him. Instead, he exhaled sharply and shrugged. "At least I know where the trexium comes from." He could feel the weight of their stares, the silent assessment in their eyes. To them, he was just another expendable laborer, another set of hands meant for hauling rock. But for the first time, they didn't immediately dismiss him. A few of them exchanged glances, as if reconsidering their assumptions. One soldier cleared his throat in the uncomfortable silence that followed.

"Guess I never thought about it that way," he admitted, rubbing the back of his neck. Another muttered something under his breath but didn't push back.

Revik smirked. "See? Even grunts can learn something." He gave Cal a light clap on the shoulder. "Don't let it go to your head, Miner, but you might not be completely useless after all."

Varek stood near the perimeter, arms folded, watching the exercises with an unreadable expression. The Vanguard remained near him, silent and imposing. Cal noticed subtle differences in their armor—some bulkier, others more streamlined.

As the soldiers dispersed back to their routines, Cal turned his attention fully toward the Vanguard. The difference between them and the standard soldiers was stark. Where the recruits moved with effort, the Vanguard moved with practiced efficiency, their steps measured, their reactions sharp. It was like watching an entirely different breed of warrior.

Revik caught him staring and smirked. "Different, aren't they? There's a reason they lead the charge. Standard soldiers hold the line. The Vanguard break it." Revik nodded toward them. "That's Daryas, the one on the left. She leads the War Angels, they're a team of five. The best. She's deadly in close combat. You see the black armor with the purple streak? That's her signature. The one next to her? Smokey—her partner, and a damn good shot. His armor's a dull grey, earned the name because he moves like smoke, always slipping in and out before you can pin him down. The deep green armor? That's Cab. Heavy-hitter, brute force fighter. Grassie's the small one, the fastest of them— yellowish tint on her armor. She's got a reputation for outrunning just about anything, and word is she joined up just to keep getting access to good food. And then there's Rich, the big one. Takes shots that would put most people down and keeps moving. Not the fastest, but when he's in the fight, he doesn't stop."

Cal studied them with renewed intensity, taking in every detail of their armor, the way they moved. They weren't just elite—they carried themselves like people who knew they would outlast anyone who stood against them.

"And the names?" Cal asked after a moment. "They all mean something?"

Revik smirked. "Most of 'em. Some earn their names in the field, others get stuck with them for dumber reasons. Smokey picked his up early on—moves like a ghost, vanishes when things get too hot. Grassie? She got hers 'cause she talks about food more than anything else. First week in the barracks, she wouldn't shut up about fresh vegetables. Kept saying she'd kill for a patch of green. Kept talking about something called Matcha," Revik shrugged. "Stuck ever since."

Cal chuckled, shaking his head. "Not what I expected."

"It never is," Revik said. "But that's the Vanguard for you."

The soldiers, for their part still seemed to regard him as unworthy of their time, or even their presence for that matter. They scoffed and jeered at him when they had time between battles, needling him for some kind of reaction.

Revik studied Cal for a moment, noting his lack of response, then let out a low chuckle.

"Huh. You got some fight in you, Miner. Maybe Varek's onto something."

Cal nodded slowly, absorbing every detail as the Vanguard members began to spar. Unlike the recruits, who hesitated and second-guessed their movements, the Vanguard struck without hesitation. Each attack was precise, each counter effortless. And standing just beyond the training pit, Varek watched it all, unmoving, his arms crossed over his chest.

At one point, another officer approached him, speaking in low tones. Varek barely responded, his gaze never leaving the training pit. Whatever had been said, it wasn't worth breaking focus. Every so often, he gave a small nod, signaling to an instructor, making note of performances, absorbing every detail like a man who had already calculated a dozen outcomes before anyone else had even considered the first.

An instructor barked orders, sending two recruits into a sparring ring while the others formed a loop around them to watch.

He didn't belong here. But he wanted to.

He forced himself to stay still, to not let the tension in his shoulders betray his thoughts. Watching wasn't a privilege. It was a test.

And if Varek was watching him as closely as he was watching the soldiers, he needed to prove that he could keep up.

But he already knew.

This was where he was meant to be.

Chapter 5 - Orders to Move

The first sign was always subtle—an extra layer of tension in the air, whispers among the quartermasters, supply shipments slowing down. Then, the storm hit. Orders barked across the stronghold. Crates stacked in perfect rows, waiting to be loaded. The clatter of tools dismantling barricades, boots stomping over packed dirt.

Every three to four months, it happened. The stronghold was never permanent, never meant to be. The walls that had sheltered them would soon be torn down, leaving nothing but dust in their wake. And just when people started to feel like they belonged, the call came.

Time to move.

Cal had found a rhythm. The mines by day, training grounds by night. At first, he had only watched, standing at the edges, memorizing the way soldiers moved, how orders flowed down the chain. Then Varek had started slipping him supply lists—at first without explanation, then later with a single, quiet expectation.

The first time, it had been a test. The second, a challenge. Now, it was routine. He tracked shipments, cross-checked manifests, saw the flow of resources that kept the stronghold alive. It wasn't just numbers on paper anymore. He was starting to see it—the machine behind survival.

Rumors spread first—talk of a break in the weather, an opening at the mountain's edge, a chance to move before the next seasonal shift closed the pass again. The first confirmation came when supply shipments were halted, and non-essential work was suspended. Then, the real order arrived. It was expected, yet always unwelcome. Every three to four months, they packed up their lives, leaving behind whatever fragile sense of permanence they had built. The stronghold was designed for mobility, its foundations temporary, its walls meant to be broken down and rebuilt elsewhere. Just as the people started to feel like they belonged, the order came. Time to go.

The stronghold pulsed with movement—orders shouted, crates packed, weapons checked and rechecked. Cal barely had time to process it before a runner grabbed his arm. "Varek wants you."

He found the commander standing over a table covered in maps, red markers cutting across terrain lines, marking routes and danger zones. The relocation wasn't just about resources. It never was. The climate shifted, food ran low, but that wasn't what forced them out.

Something always did.

The undead pressing too close. A faction moving in. An outbreak spiraling beyond control. It never mattered how long they lasted. The result was always the same.

It had started a few weeks prior, the signs subtle at first. More frequent patrols. Small attacks on the perimeter—zombies that hadn't been there before suddenly appearing in clusters. Then, the bigger issue: the trexium mines were becoming unstable. The deeper they dug, the more collapses occurred. Accidents increased. And just like that, the decision was made for them. It was time to move, but they always had to wait for a break in the weather.

Every new place brought its own challenges, new dangers they had to overcome. Last time, it had been a lack of metal ore, forcing them to strip vehicles and melt down what little salvage they could find. This time? No one knew yet. That was the real fear—the unknown. It always waited for them. The halls were filled with movement, soldiers reinforcing supply caravans, engineers double-checking vehicles, and quartermasters barking orders as crates of weapons and rations were accounted for. The entire base was shifting gears, transitioning from a place of endurance to one of movement. It was efficient, almost too efficient. The way everything packed up so neatly, the way no trace was left behind. The stronghold had functioned here for months, but within a matter of days, it would be as if they had never lived here at all. The land would be empty, the tunnels sealed, the barricades torn down. Another empty ruin waiting to be swallowed by time. Or something else. It was as if they had never been there at all. Cal had never questioned it before, but now, something about it made the hairs on the back of his neck stand up.

Cal entered Varek's office to find the commander standing over a large table, maps spread across its surface. Various markers and notes covered the terrain, outlining paths through the mountain pass and anticipated trouble spots. Varek barely looked up.

"Sit," he ordered. Cal did, noting the group of soldiers he found saw lining the walls of the room.

For a long moment, Varek studied him. "You've been watching, listening, putting things together. Now it's time for something real."

Cal frowned. "You mean the move."

"Exactly." Varek tapped the map. "We move at dawn. I want the first supply convoys packed and prepared within the hour."

"Just like that, huh?"

The voice came from the back, gruff, heavy with years spent watching strongholds rise and fall. A veteran stood with his arms crossed, gaze sharp. "Pack up and run again?"

Another soldier shifted his weight, glancing between the officers. "Feels like we're always running. What's the point of fortifying if we never stay long enough to hold it?"

No one answered right away. But the silence said enough.

A few others nodded, their unease growing. Even the officers exchanged looks.

Varek didn't flinch. He let the tension build before speaking. "I'm not asking you to like it. I'm telling you to do it." His gaze swept the room, pinning each soldier in place. "Or would you rather stay behind and find out why every damn stronghold moves? See what waits for you when you get left behind?"

Silence.

A few exchanged glances but said nothing. Then, slowly, they started to move—grumbling, hesitating, but following orders.

Varek exhaled, low and quiet, before muttering under his breath. "That's what I thought."

Cal couldn't help but feel like this was a show. Like they were supposed to ask those questions. Varek was supposed to respond the way he did, and Cal was supposed to play his part and accept it. The whole interaction felt… off.

Cal swallowed, scanning the maps and bringing his attention to the more immediate challenge. "And if something goes wrong?"

Varek's smirk was humorless. "Something always goes wrong. It's our job to make sure we handle it."

The stronghold unraveled like a thread being pulled from the seams.

Walls dismantled, sandbags stacked for transport, trenches filled like they had never been dug. Even the fire pits were scrubbed, the last traces of warmth smothered beneath packed earth. Cal watched as it all disappeared, methodical, practiced— not just survival. A pattern.

He swallowed hard. Why did it have to be this clean?

Equipment was loaded onto massive transports, heavy-duty vehicles designed to withstand rough terrain. Scout teams were already ahead, ensuring the route remained clear. The stronghold had been built to move, but that didn't make it easy.

Cal found himself assigned to one of the observation posts, stationed with a logistics team overseeing the convoy's organization. Joran was there too, though he didn't look happy about it.

"Of all the ways I thought we'd die, being crushed under a supply crate wasn't on my list," Joran muttered, securing a strap on a trexium transport case.

"Better than the alternative," Cal said, nodding toward the perimeter, where soldiers kept watch.

Joran sighed. "You think we'll actually make it through the pass before the next storm?"

Cal had no answer. He could only watch as the first wave of transports rumbled forward, their engines growling in the cold morning air.

Cal spotted his parents near the labor convoy, their transport half-loaded with supplies. His mother was adjusting the straps on a crate, while his father methodically checked off items on a battered clipboard. They worked in quiet efficiency, but there was a tension in their movements that hadn't been there before.

Instead of calling out, Cal approached and took a bundle of supplies, to secure it onto the flatbed. His father glanced up, then exchanged a look with his mother. They didn't need words to understand what he was doing—one last act to help before the move took them in different directions. He stepped in without a word, securing the heavy bundle onto the flatbed. It was routine, something he'd done dozens of times before. But this time, it was different.

His mother wiped her hands on her coat and turned toward him, searching his face. "Cal, you've been working yourself to the bone. You barely sleep anymore. Are you sure this is what you want?"

Cal nodded but didn't immediately answer. He tightened the last strap on the crate before meeting her gaze. "It's not about what I want, Mom. It's about what I need to do."

His father let out a slow breath, setting the clipboard down with deliberate care, like the weight of his next words was heavier than anything on that page. He didn't meet Cal's eyes at first— just ran a thumb along the edge of the worn paper before finally looking up.

"Son." A pause. Then, quieter. "I know you think this is the right path. Maybe it is. Maybe Varek sees something in you that we don't. But that doesn't matter to us."

His hand landed on Cal's shoulder, fingers firm, grounding. "You're still our boy. We don't care what title you have, what uniform you wear—we just want you safe." His grip tightened slightly, a silent plea. "You've been distant. Feels like you're already leaving us behind. Just... tell me that's not true."

Cal swallowed hard, his fingers curling into fists at his sides. "I just want to understand," he said, the words coming rough, unsteady. "How things really work. To make my own choices. To find my place here." His jaw tensed. "You always told me to keep my head down, but that's not enough. Not anymore."

His mother sighed, stepping closer. Her palm brushed his cheek, calloused but warm—the same way she had soothed him when he was young, when the world had felt simpler.

"Surviving is enough, Cal," she murmured. "You don't have to carry the weight of it all."

Cal let the moment linger before gently pulling away, offering her a small, reassuring smile. "You and Dad made sure we survived. I want to make sure we don't have to keep running forever."

His father studied him for a long moment, then placed a firm hand on his shoulder. "I may not understand why you're doing this, but I know you. You don't quit. Just promise me you'll be careful."

Cal hesitated before nodding. "I promise."

His mother touched his arm one last time, then turned toward the transport. His father gave him one last lingering look before following. Cal watched them disappear into the convoy, his heart heavy but steady. He had made his choice, but they would always be his home. Cal watched them go, feeling something tighten in his chest, but there was no time to dwell on it. He had his own assignment to get to.

The airship rocked slightly as Cal climbed aboard, the cold biting through his coat the moment he stepped onto the upper deck. He hadn't been in one of these before—hadn't realized how hollow the metal sounded beneath his boots, how the walls felt too thin against the wind outside.

The vehicle rumbled beneath them, the faint hum of trexium-powered thrusters vibrating through the metal frame. The world stretched below—mountains and wastelands, the skeletons of dead strongholds overrun by infected and abandoned.

Cal shifted, uneasy. "Feels... fragile."

A man across from him chuckled, adjusting his grip on his case. "It is."

"Not exactly reassuring," Cal muttered.

"Reassurance is for people who can afford it," the man said. His voice was lighter than his expression.

The scientist chuckled, shifting the case beside him as if making room. "Name's Corvin, by the way. Research division. You must be the one Varek's keeping an eye on."

Cal studied him for a moment before settling into his seat. "Seems like a lot of people have been watching me lately."

Corvin leered. "That's what happens when you start stepping outside your role. People take notice."

He paused, his gaze flicking to Cal in a way that felt... evaluating. "Some more than others."

Cal frowned. "What does that mean?"

"It means most people in your position don't ask questions." Corvin adjusted the case beside him, the dull metal catching the light.

Cal's pulse quickened. "And you do?"

"I notice patterns," Corvin said lightly. "And I notice the people who notice them." He exhaled, shaking his head. "You're either going to be very useful... or a very big problem."

Cal let that linger before glancing out the small window at the caravan below. "So, if you're research division, what exactly do you research?"

Corvin tapped the case beside him. "The virus. Patterns. Movement. The way things shift and change in this world. It's not just about surviving the undead—it's about understanding how this thing keeps evolving and how we finally stop it."

Cal frowned. "You think we can stop it? For good?"

Corvin exhaled, his expression unreadable. "That's the goal, isn't it? Otherwise, what's the point of all this?"

Cal's eyes drifted toward the metal case beside Corvin. It was sturdy, reinforced at the corners, and locked tight. Not standard field equipment. "What's in the case?"

Corvin's smirk returned, but this time it didn't quite reach his eyes. "Classified. You wouldn't find it all that interesting, anyway."

Cal raised an eyebrow. "Then why bring it?"

Corvin leaned back, stretching his legs slightly. "Because some things are too important to leave behind. Just like you, I imagine."

Cal studied him for a moment, weighing his words as he thought about the logistics of the move. He had the chance to ask all the questions he had wondered since he was a boy. "Why don't we just fly over the mountains?" Cal asked, glancing out the narrow window. "Seems easier than waiting for a pass to open."

Corvin smirked, but it didn't reach his eyes. "You think we haven't tried?" He leaned back slightly, fingers tapping absently against the metal case beside him. "Every time we've sent an airship over, it never comes back. Doesn't matter how much trexium we pump into the engines, how reinforced the hull is. No wreckage. No distress signals."

Cal's stomach dipped. "Nothing?"

Corvin's smirk faded. "No one knows what's on the other side of the larger mountains." A pause. Then, quieter—"No one still alive, anyway."

Corvin allowed for a short silence to fall between them before continuing.

"That's why we follow the passes. The storms break in cycles, and when they do, we move. It's the only way forward."

Cal exhaled, staring out the small window at the clouds shifting around them. "And what causes the storms?"

"Good question." Corvin's voice was casual, but his expression wasn't. Corvin didn't seem to think that an answer to his question was warranted.

The airship jolted slightly as it adjusted course, and Corvin looked toward the cockpit, as if reading something in the shift of their trajectory. Cal sat back, letting the conversation settle in his mind. There were too many questions, too many half-answers that only led to more mystery. But one thing was certain—this move wasn't just about escaping the undead or finding more resources. Something else was at play, and Cal had a feeling he was only beginning to see the edges of it.

Chapter 6 – Wings of the Undead

The airship hummed beneath Cal's boots, vibrations running through the metal floor as it sliced through the sky. Below, the ground churned, rolling views over the wasteland like shifting tides. From up here, the world looked still. Deceptively still.

But Cal knew better.

The ground below wasn't empty—it was a graveyard of people lost in this round of the valley. Most strongholds made it out, but you couldn't help but notice the wreckage of the ones that didn't.

He sat near the observation window, his fingers gripping the armrest tighter than he wanted to admit. Across from him, Corvin was hunched over his case, adjusting the locks. Varek stood near the cockpit, speaking with the pilot in low tones. The airship rattled slightly as the wind shifted.

"You've got that first-time flier grip on the seat," Corvin remarked, barely glancing up from his case.

Cal forced his fingers to unclench. "Not on something this small. Feels like one good gust could rip us out of the sky."

Corvin chuckled. "Well, try not to think about it. And if you do fall—aim for something soft."

Cal opened his mouth to respond, but the cockpit comms crackled to life.

"Movement on the outer edge of the storm—looks like—" The rest was swallowed by static, then a sharp curse.

"Damn it. We've got flyers."

Varek's head, listening to Cal and Corvin's conversation impassively, snapped toward the windshield. "How many?"

"At least a dozen. Maybe more. They're coming fast."

The airship veered slightly, and Cal caught sight of them through the window—dark figures gliding through the sky, their massive wings beating against the wind. Their bodies were twisted mockeries of what they once were, their flesh stretched too thin over elongated limbs, their mouths lined with jagged, uneven teeth.

Zombie flyers.

"Missile teams, get ready!" Varek barked into his comm. "Take them down before they get too close."

Outside, the escort ships adjusted formation. Vanguard missile specialists took their positions, launching precise bursts of firepower into the oncoming horde. Explosions lit up the sky, shredding some of the creatures instantly, but others kept coming, maneuvering unpredictably through the air.

Then, the airship jolted violently.

"Shit! We've been hit!" the pilot shouted. "Portside engine's failing!"

The airship lurched. A violent, stomach-dropping tilt that sent Cal's head snapping to the side. The only thing keeping him from slamming into the bulkhead was the seat restraints digging into his chest.

Across from him, Corvin's case crashed to the floor, the impact popping the lid just enough to expose what lay inside—a sliver of metal, smooth and shining with a dim, unnatural glow from the light pouring in through the windows.

Corvin swore, unstrapped himself, lunged to snap it shut, his hands moving faster than Cal had ever seen. He grabbed up the case and strapped himself back in.

A screech ripped through the air—a wet, grating sound that clawed down the spine like nails against metal. The airship shuddered beneath them, the hull groaning as something massive latched onto the side.

"We've got contact!" someone shouted.

The gunner at the side door leaned out, opening fire, muzzle flashes cutting through the storm. Cal caught a glimpse of something—not quite human anymore—its wings stretched wide, leathery and unnatural, its eyes fogged over with the sickly glow of infection.

The impact sent a shockwave through the cabin, but the second one broke them.

Something massive crashed into the hull—metal shrieked as it gave, ripping open like tin under a hammer. The airship bucked violently, throwing Cal sideways. His shoulder slammed against the bulkhead, pain flashing white-hot before alarms screeched to life.

Red warning lights stuttered across the cabin. Decompression alerts flashed. A rush of air tore through the breach.

Then the ship plunged.

Metal shrieked as the airship tilted, weight jerking sideways as alarms blared—warning lights flashing red, red, red. The floor vanished beneath him.

Wind roared in his ears. He barely registered the shouting before gravity took over, ripping him from the wreckage.

He was falling.

For one horrifying second, he was weightless. Then the open sky swallowed him whole.

The world became wind and weightlessness.

Cal tumbled through the open air, the airship spinning into the storm above him. He barely heard the shouts—only the howling wind, the violent pull of gravity, the distant pulse of fire and wreckage.

His limbs flailed uselessly. No control. No direction. Only the ground, rising up too fast—

Then, nothing.

Consciousness dragged him back in pieces. A dull, throbbing pain. The taste of copper in his mouth. The slow realization that he was still breathing.

Cal groaned, rolling onto his side. The world tilted, nausea clawing at his gut as he pushed himself up on shaking arms. His limbs protested, stiff and aching, but nothing was broken. Somehow.

Leaves crunched beneath him. Branches. Vines. A dense canopy loomed overhead, thick with tangled limbs that had, impossibly, kept him from becoming part of the ground.

The air smelled of smoke. Burning metal. Something worse.

Through the canopy, the sky pulsed with flickering orange, the last remnants of wreckage still burning somewhere in the distance. Gunfire crackled, faint but steady, echoing across the treetops.

But closer—too close—something shifted.

A sound, sickeningly almost human.

A wet, guttural groan.

Don't move.

Cal's breath hitched as his gaze followed the sound.

Not ten feet away, a figure dragged itself through the underbrush. Its limbs twitched with unnatural jerks, its head lolling at an angle no living thing could survive. Skin, ruined and torn, clung in strips to exposed muscle.

The groan came again, rattling, breathless. Then another.

Not just one.

More figures emerged from the underbrush, their movements jerky and unnatural. Some still bore the remnants of their former lives—tattered clothing, rusted armor plates, even remnants of weapons fused into their decaying flesh. Their sunken eyes locked onto him, and for a moment, they hesitated, as if processing the new presence among them.

Cal's breath hitched. He had seen the aftermath of zombie attacks, had heard the stories whispered in the barracks. But this was different. This was real. And he was alone.

He forced himself to move, pushing through the pain radiating from his ribs. He needed to get to higher ground, get a weapon—anything. His hands searched the ground blindly until they closed around a broken tree branch, jagged at the tip. It wasn't much, but it was better than nothing.

The closest zombie lurched forward, a gurgling moan escaping its ruined throat. Cal took a step back, his heartbeat thundering in his ears. Then another step. He couldn't fight them all. Running was the only option.

His body reacted before his mind did.

He ran.

Branches lashed at his skin. Vines snagged at his boots. The forest was thick, damp, and suffocating, every breath ragged in his throat. But behind him—

More movement.

The shuffle of uneven steps. The snap of undergrowth crushed beneath twisted feet.

The world was trees and breath and pounding blood—until something else cut through it.

Voices.

Not them. Not that rattling, breathless groan. Not the wet sound of dragging limbs.

This was sharp. Controlled. Human.

The gunfire didn't come immediately. Cal kept running, weaving through the trees, his lungs burning as the infected pursued him. He risked a glance back—there were more than he'd thought, too many. His grip tightened on the useless stick in his hands. He wasn't going to outrun them forever.

Then, just as his strength began to wane, the night itself seemed to split apart. A thunderous crack echoed through the forest, the muzzle flash of high-caliber rounds illuminating the darkness like lightning. One of the zombies' heads exploded mid-step, its body collapsing in a heap. A second shot, a third—each a perfect, calculated kill. The air filled with the unmistakable scent of burning propellant as heavy rounds ripped through decayed flesh.

Then they arrived.

The Vanguard emerged from the shadows like wraiths, moving with terrifying precision. Daryas was first, her purple-streaked armor catching the dim light as she strode forward with fluid ease, rifle raised, scanning for more threats. Behind her, Smokey flickered between cover, his dull gray armor blending into the surroundings as he lined up his next shot in perfect synchronization with Daryas'. Cab moved methodically, her deep green plating almost black in the dark, every step measured as she fired controlled bursts into the advancing infected. Grassie vaulted over a fallen log, moving like liquid shadow, her yellow-tinted armor barely catching the moonlight.

And then came Rich. He was a living wall, his armor reinforced for close combat. One of the zombies lunged for him, but he didn't even flinch. His massive arm shot out, catching the creature by the throat before he crushed its windpipe with a sickening crunch. A second later, his sidearm barked once, putting it down permanently.

Cal barely had time to process it. One moment he was running for his life—the next, the zombies were nothing but lifeless husks on the ground, the only sound left in the clearing the soft clicks of Vanguard rifles being reloaded.

Cal could do nothing but watch, heart pounding, breath ragged. The display of raw, calculated efficiency was unlike anything he had ever seen. These weren't just soldiers—they were forces of nature, the embodiment of everything he had ever dreamed of becoming.

Then, as swiftly as it had begun, the battle was over. The clearing fell silent, the air thick with the acrid scent of blood and gunpowder. The only sounds were the occasional twitch of a still-dying corpse and the quiet clicks of Vanguard rifles being reloaded.

"Got him! Keep moving!"

Daryas' voice was sharp, cutting through the chaos like a blade. She moved without hesitation, rifle still hot from the last shot, scanning the trees for more threats.

As the last body fell, Smokey looked at Cal, hands on his knees still working to catch his breath.

"You look like hell."

Cal staggered, breath heaving. A half-laugh, half-disbelieving exhale slipped from his lips as he gestured behind him to the fallen bodies of his pursuers.

"You should see the other guys."

The rest of the team spread out, securing the perimeter. Smokey, in his dull gray armor, kept his rifle raised, scanning for movement. Cab adjusted her stance beside him, her deep green plating standing out even in the darkness. Grassie, the smallest of the group, moved with an eerie silence, her yellow-tinged armor barely making a sound as she checked the surroundings. And then there was Rich, his frame towering over the others, his weapon looking almost comically small in his grip.

Cal swallowed hard. "How did you—?"

"We've been searching for you for hours," Daryas said, slinging her rifle over her shoulder. "Varek gave us a three-hour window to find you, but the convoy had to move on. You almost missed your window."

Daryas muttered, eyes scanning the trees. "We were about to call it when you popped up on motion sensors."

Cal's breath hitched. The exhaustion sank deeper.

"They... left?"

Smokey gave him a sidelong glance. "Convoy couldn't stop for one person. Command made the call."

Cal's stomach twisted, but he forced himself to nod. There was no time for shock. He was still alive. That had to count for something.

Daryas tossed him a spare sidearm. Cal caught it awkwardly, nearly fumbling it before tightening his grip. It felt heavier than he expected, the weight unfamiliar in his hands. He had seen weapons like this before—he had helped load crates of them back at the supply depot—but holding one himself was different.

His fingers searched for the safety, his grip unsure. He had seen soldiers work their weapons with fluid ease, but for him, it was a clumsy struggle. He fumbled with the slide, trying to chamber a round, but the mechanism resisted.

Smokey sighed, stepping closer. "Miner, you planning to shoot your own foot, or do you want some help?"

Cal shot him a glare, but it lacked real heat. "I've handled plenty of these before."

"Sure you have." Smokey reached over, adjusting Cal's grip with practiced ease before flicking the safety off for him. "Try not to freeze up when you actually need to pull the trigger."

Daryas smirked. "Good. Then you can help us get back. Because we're not alone out here, and something bigger is coming."

No hesitation. No wasted movement.

The Vanguards pulled him forward, weaving through the trees with practiced precision. Weapons raised, heads on a swivel. Their boots barely made a sound against the damp forest floor.

Cal had never moved like this before—every step felt too loud, every breath too ragged. The underbrush was thick, clawing at his legs, but the Vanguard never slowed.

Cal did his best to keep up, trying not to slow them down past the aches and pains from his fall, not to mention their quick movements and high endurance.

The trees thinned, giving way to open ground—dry, cracked earth pockmarked with old craters. The smell of burned metal and decay clung to the air. Ahead, the ruins of a stronghold loomed in the fog, its broken skeleton half-swallowed by mist.

Vehicles sat abandoned, doors yawning open, interiors gutted. The wind shifted, carrying the distant creak of something rusted moving in the breeze.

"That our path?" Cal asked, nodding toward the ruined skyline.

"It's the fastest way to intercept the convoy," Smokey said. "Unless you feel like walking an extra fifty miles through dense trees like we just came through."

Cal sighed.

"Didn't think so," said Smokey smugly.

Daryas held up a fist, and everyone stopped. She pointed to a collapsed overpass in the distance. "That's where we need to go. If the convoy stayed on schedule, they passed through there not long ago. We'll track their trail from there."

"There's movement in the ruins," Grassie murmured, crouching near the edge of the road. She tapped the side of her helmet, her motion scanner picking up heat signatures beyond the ruins. "A lot of movement."

"How bad?" Cab asked, shifting her grip on her weapon.

Grassie exhaled. "Bad."

Chapter 7 – Through Ash and Ruin

The Vanguard retreated to higher ground, moving with practiced efficiency as they put distance between themselves and the overrun stronghold below. The skyline stretched out before them, an eerie maze of skeletal buildings and rusting vehicles. Smoke still lingered in the air, remnants of past destruction. From their vantage point, Cal could see the full extent of the devastation—and the danger.

They reached a rocky ridge overlooking the ruined stronghold, its jagged terrain giving them a clear vantage point without exposing them too much. Below them stretched the remnants of what had once been a stronghold, its defensive walls shattered, watchtowers collapsed, and structures either burned out or overrun. Abandoned barricades, rusting vehicles, and makeshift fortifications lay in ruin, now claimed by the dead. Fires still smoldered from distant wreckage, casting an eerie glow over the chaos.

Daryas took a knee, pulling out a small pair of binoculars. "We'll hole up here for a bit, get a read on the stronghold before we try to move."

Cal stepped forward, drawn toward the edge of the ridge. The view was overwhelming. He could see the movement of the infected, how they ebbed and flowed through the streets like a tide, clustering in broken alleyways and open courtyards. He turned to walk to see things from a slightly different angle.

A distant *boom* rattled the air.

Cal stopped mid-step. The ground beneath him *trembled*, a slow, rolling vibration that settled in his bones. Then, through the haze of dust and smoke, a shape emerged—massive, lumbering, unnatural.

Grave Titan.

The monster moved in a slow, deliberate march, its rotting frame reinforced with twisted metal plating. It was heading straight for the ruins. Straight for them.

It marched forward, its grotesque form illuminated by the smoldering fires of the ruined base. The behemoth moved with slow, earthshaking steps, each one sending tremors through the ruined streets. At this pace, it would reach the heart of the stronghold in twenty minutes—drawn, no doubt, by the vibrations of the convoy that had passed through before them. Smaller zombies scattered in its wake, instinctively avoiding the thing's path, as if even the undead feared it.

Cal exhaled slowly. If they were going to get through the stronghold, they had to do it before that thing arrived—or make damn sure they didn't draw its attention.

Behind him, the Vanguard had already started discussing their next move, their voices low but urgent. Daryas suggested circling wide to avoid the densest parts of the horde. Smokey wanted to find a high point and scout for alternative routes. Cab argued that they should wait and observe longer before making a decision.

Cal listened, his eyes still fixed on the shifting masses below. The undead weren't random—there was a rhythm to them, an order hidden in the chaos. He saw gaps, weak points in the way they clustered, potential paths that could be exploited. His fingers curled into his palms.

They weren't seeing it.

"I think I have a plan!" he cut in, his voice sharper than he intended. The group quieted, their attention shifting to him. He cleared his throat and turned toward them. "We don't need to fight our way through. We need to use the way they move against them."

Smokey looked at him skeptically. "Yeah? What, we just walk through the front door and hope they don't notice?"

He hesitated for half a second before saying, "Walking through the front door is a bad idea... usually." He glanced up, catching Daryas' slight smirk, and then pressed on. "We don't need to force our way in—we make them move where we want instead. No," Cal said, shaking his head. "Look at the way they move. They're not just aimless. They react to sound, to movement—but not all at once. If we use that, we can create distractions to keep them off us. We'll split their attention and move in teams, using the wreckage as cover."

Daryas crossed her arms. "And how exactly do you propose we do that? We don't have an army at our backs."

Cal crouched, using a piece of broken concrete to map out the stronghold layout in the dust. "We use what's already here. Look—this section of the stronghold tower is unstable. If we time it right, we can trigger a collapse on the east side, drawing the bulk of the undead that way. Then we move through this route here—staying low, using the wreckage to keep out of sight. It's a straight shot to the front gates, and if we move fast, we'll be out before the undead even realize we were there, cutting right through the center without having to go all the way around."

The group was silent as they studied the rough map. Grassie let out a low whistle. "That's... not bad."

Cab nodded. "Actually, it might work."

Rich cracked his knuckles. "It's risky. But we've pulled off worse."

Daryas studied Cal for a long moment before nodding. "Alright, Miner. We'll do it your way."

Smokey arched a brow. "Since when do we take orders from a miner?"

Daryas chuckled. "Since he came up with a better plan than you did."

Cal straightened slightly, feeling the weight of their attention on him. For the first time, they weren't just looking at him as a stray worker who needed rescuing. They saw something else— something even he hadn't realized was there.

"Alright," Daryas said, standing. "We move now. We don't have time to waste."

The Vanguard moved swiftly, breaking into a formation that kept them spread out but within line of sight of one another. Every step was calculated, their footfalls carefully placed to avoid loose debris that could give away their position. The wind howled through the skeletal remains of buildings, rattling rusted signs and sending scattered papers skittering across the ground. Cal's heart pounded as they pressed forward, the cold air biting at his exposed skin.

Daryas signaled for them to halt, pressing her back against a crumbling wall. She peered around the corner, scanning the pathway ahead before gesturing for them to move again. The stronghold was massive—bigger than Cal had expected—and its twisted ruins stretched further than their eyes could see in every direction. This place was nearly three times the size of their own stronghold, but that hadn't seemed to matter. What had once been reinforced barricades and heavily defended structures now lay in ruin, overrun by the dead.

As they crept through an abandoned checkpoint, Cal noticed the remains of a last stand—empty casings littered the ground, scorch marks blackened the walls, and broken rifles lay beside skeletal figures slumped against the sandbags. The people stationed here had fought until the very end. And lost.

The Vanguard team, which Cal recognized as the War Angels moved in tight formation, shadows slipping between rusted wreckage and scorched-out bunkers. Abandoned supply crates littered the streets, some splintered open, their contents long picked clean. Others remained sealed—untouched, forgotten, or ignored.

The deeper they went, the thicker the air became, choked with the distant, rattling moans of the dead. Their plan was working—the explosion had pulled most of them east. But that didn't mean the ones left behind were any less dangerous.

A section of collapsed roadway forced them into a tight corridor between two ruined buildings. The air was thick with the stench of decay, and the tension in the group was palpable.

Then came the first real problem.

The first one snapped its head toward them at the sound of shifting rock, its hollow eyes locking onto movement. Then it lunged.

More emerged from the rubble, dragging broken limbs, pulling themselves free from the ruins faster than Cal expected. Too fast.

"Contact!" Smokey hissed, already raising his rifle.

Daryas didn't hesitate. "Suppressing fire—short bursts! Keep moving!"

Gunfire erupted in controlled bursts, the dull pink glow of trexium charging through the Vanguard rifles as they tore into the approaching undead. Cal stumbled back as one of the creatures lunged at him, its fingers clawing for his throat. His hand fumbled for his weapon, too slow, the thing's breath hot and rotten against his face—

Then impact.

Cab's boot slammed into its chest, sending it hurtling backward. It crashed into a heap of rusted steel, limbs twitching, convulsing, before it stilled.

"Keep your head on a swivel, Miner!" she barked, pulling him back to his feet.

They sprinted through the wreckage, dodging debris and maneuvering through the skeletal remains of old buildings. The distraction plan was working—the undead were still moving toward the eastern collapse they had triggered. But the noise they had made was drawing smaller hordes in unpredictable ways. Every gunshot, every movement threatened to send the delicate balance spiraling out of control.

Then came the real problem.

The Grave Titan had arrived.

The ground trembled beneath its massive weight as it entered the stronghold's core, its hollow eyes scanning its surroundings. The creature moved with unnatural purpose, sniffing the air, searching. Then, it turned toward them.

The Vanguard pressed against the remains of a burnt-out transport vehicle, watching as the behemoth lumbered through the ruins. It was closer now—much closer than they wanted. Its skeletal frame was reinforced with jagged metal, pieces of old-world machinery fused into its decayed flesh. The sight of it sent a cold shiver down Cal's spine.

"We can't outrun that thing," Cab muttered.

Cal's mind raced. They had to finish what they started. "The tower," Cal blurted out, pointing. "We bring it down on top of it."

Daryas' head snapped toward him, then toward the skeletal structure leaning precariously over the battlefield. She was quiet for a beat, then her stance shifted—weight settling on one hip, head tilting slightly.

"Alright, Miner." A smirk ghosted through her voice. "Let's see if you're as smart as you think you are."

The team shifted course, setting up their final maneuver. They needed to lure the Grave Titan into position, but that meant exposing themselves long enough to get its attention.

"Grassie, you're fastest," Daryas said. "You make it mad. We bring it down."

Grassie let out a long exhale. "Great. Bait duty. Love that for me."

Then she was gone. A blur of motion as she sprinted into the open, boots kicking up dust, rifle snapping up—two precise shots into the Grave Titan's exposed ribs.

The creature froze. Twitched. Then its massive head swung toward her, hollow sockets locking on.

Then it moved.

The roar split the air like a bomb, deep, guttural, deafening. The ground trembled as it charged.

"Move, move, move!" Daryas ordered, the team scattering into position as Grassie led the monstrosity into the kill zone.

The ground quaked with every step it took, its massive arms swiping through abandoned vehicles as if they were weightless. Grassie barely stayed ahead, using the wreckage to keep distance between herself and the creature's relentless pursuit.

Meanwhile, the rest of the team set the explosives at the base of the tower, working fast as the creature barreled toward them.

"Charges set!" Cab called out. "Grassie, bring it in!"

Grassie made a hard turn, sprinting toward the tower just as the titan lunged for her. She dove at the last second, rolling out of the way as the behemoth collided with the unstable structure.

"Blow it!" Daryas snapped.

Smokey didn't hesitate.

The click of the detonator was drowned out by the instant eruption of fire and stone. A shockwave ripped through the battlefield as the explosion tore into the tower's foundations.

Cracks splintered upward.

The Grave Titan staggered, confused—then realized too late.

The tower gave a deep, tortured groan as gravity took over. Stone collapsed inward, the roar of destruction swallowing the monster's final bellow before it was buried beneath tons of rubble.

Silence followed, save for the settling dust and the faint crackling of fire.

Daryas exhaled, shaking her head. "Well, Miner. That actually worked."

Cal exhaled sharply, wiping sweat from his brow with a shaking hand. His heart still pounded in his ribs, but the dust was settling. The tower was gone.

So was the Titan.

"Yeah," he muttered, voice hoarse. "I figured it would."

Smokey let out a dry, breathless laugh. "You *figured.*"

Daryas clapped him on the back. "Alright, let's get moving before something worse shows up. We've got a stronghold to get through."

The team regrouped, moving swiftly toward their next objective. The battle wasn't over yet—but they had won this round.

And Cal had just proven himself in a way none of them had expected.

As they advanced, a collapsed roadway forced them into a tight corridor between two ruined buildings. It was there that they encountered the first pack of undead, their grotesque forms spilling out of the rubble like ants disturbed from a nest.

"Damn it!" Smokey hissed, raising his rifle. "We need to move faster."

"No time to waste ammo!" Daryas ordered. "Stick to the plan, let them run to the wreckage! Keep moving!"

They sprinted through the wreckage, navigating debris and maneuvering through the skeletal remains of old buildings. The distraction plan was working—the undead were still moving toward the eastern collapse they had triggered. But the noise they had made was drawing smaller hordes in unpredictable ways.

A new wave of undead began to gather, drawn to the echoes of the explosion and their movement. Some crawled from beneath overturned vehicles, while others staggered out of collapsed buildings, their milky eyes locking onto the group. The Vanguard adjusted their formation, keeping their movements sharp and deliberate, but the path ahead was becoming a bottleneck.

"This isn't good," Grassie muttered. "We're getting funneled."

Daryas halted the group just before a narrow alleyway leading to an open courtyard. The place was a mess—scattered debris, broken barricades, and worse, a group of undead milling about, blocking their way forward. To make matters worse, behind them, the infected they'd drawn were catching up fast.

"We can't get bogged down here," Cab said, gripping her weapon. "We need a route through fast."

Cal's mind raced, eyes darting over their surroundings. Then he saw it—an old transport truck, half-buried beneath fallen debris. The stronghold's inner wall was just beyond it, and if they could create a new opening—

"We blow that truck," Cal said, pointing. "It'll take out part of the barricade and scatter the infected. We push through while they're stunned."

Smokey let out a dry chuckle. "Blow the truck? We just used the last of our charges on the tower."

"Then we improvise," Cal shot back. He was already moving, dashing toward a fallen crate of discarded weapons and equipment. He pried the lid open, sifting through it. His heart pounded as he found what he needed—several canisters of pressurized fuel, likely meant for transport vehicles. He yanked two out and carried them to the truck.

"Grab the others and help me!" He shouted.

They did, grabbing all of the fuel canisters and positioning them right where Cal had instructed. Cab and Daryas picking off the infected as they made their way into the courtyard. Cal and the others made their way to the opposite side and got cover behind a barricade.

"Smokey, you're the best shot here," Cal said, panting. "You see that fuel line exposed on the side? Hit it."

Smokey hesitated, but only for an instant. He adjusted his rifle, steadied his breathing, and squeezed the trigger.

The bullet tore through the canisters.

The explosion that followed sent a shockwave through the courtyard, fire erupting in a rolling burst that knocked several undead off their feet. The barricade crumbled, leaving a gaping hole just wide enough for them to push through.

"Move!" Daryas barked.

The team bolted forward, cutting through the dazed undead, using the smoke and fire as cover. Cal barely registered the figures grasping for him, his focus locked on the gap ahead.

They made it through, stumbling past the flames and into the next section of the stronghold.

Breathing hard, Daryas turned to Cal. "That was either reckless or brilliant."

Cal exhaled. "Both?"

Smokey smirked. "Alright, Miner. Looks like you just saved our asses again."

"Let's not get comfortable," Cab warned, scanning the distance. "We're not safe yet."

But for the first time since they'd entered the stronghold, they had a clear path forward. They just had to make it to the other side, and they were more than half way through.

Chapter 8 – The War Angels

The adrenaline was finally wearing off. The night had been nothing but movement—running, fighting, and thinking faster than Cal ever had in his life. Now that they had made it through the stronghold and into relative safety, exhaustion weighed down on his limbs like iron shackles.

They had found shelter in the remains of an old trading hub, a fortified structure once used to coordinate supply runs. The building was mostly intact, its walls reinforced by years of desperate repairs. It had likely been abandoned in a hurry, judging by the untouched supply crates still stacked against one of the inner walls. The group had taken refuge in a section of the depot that still had a working door, barricading it as best they could while they recovered.

The silence was unsettling. After the chaos of the stronghold, the lack of gunfire, roaring undead, and collapsing buildings felt unnatural.

Cal sat against the wall, rolling his sore shoulder, his body aching in ways he hadn't felt before. He had spent his entire life mining, but this? This was different. Mining was exhausting, but it was predictable. This had been a frantic fight for survival, and now his muscles felt like they had been wrung dry.

Daryas pulled off her helmet with a *sharp hiss of released pressure*, running a hand through her sweat-dampened hair. One by one, the others followed.

Smokey was last. He hesitated a beat longer than the rest, then yanked his helmet free—revealing a jagged scar that carved down his right eye, the skin tight and pale with age. It hadn't blinded him, but it had come close.

Grassie shook out her hair, her sharp features splitting into an exhausted but familiar smirk—the kind of expression that said she'd been through worse and had the stories to prove it.

Cab set her helmet down carefully, rolling her stiff shoulders. Her cropped hair did little to soften the cool, assessing look in her eyes. She watched more than she spoke.

The only one who didn't remove his helmet was Rich. He sat back against the crate, arms crossed, his visor reflecting the dim light of the depot. After a moment, Grassie raised a brow. "You ever gonna take that thing off in the field?"

Rich shifted slightly but didn't respond. Smokey let out a quiet chuckle. "Nah, let him be. He likes the mystery."

Daryas moved to sit with the rest of them, her dark hair damp with sweat, the purple streak still visible even in the dim light. She wiped her face with a cloth before glancing at Cal. "You did good, Miner."

Cal looked up at her, surprised. He expected a sarcastic remark, some kind of jab, but her tone was genuine. "Thanks. I just... did what made sense."

"That's the difference between surviving and leading," she replied. "Some people wait for orders. Others see what needs to be done and do it."

He let the words settle, unsure how to respond. Was that what he was doing? Leading?

Smokey leaned against a crate, rubbing his temple. "Alright, can we all agree that was a little too close for comfort? I mean, we just took down a Grave Titan. That's something, right?"

"It's more than something," Cab said, stretching out her legs. "That was the kind of thing people tell stories about."

"Yeah, well, let's hope we live long enough to hear one of them," Grassie muttered, leaning back with a heavy sigh. "I need at least twelve hours of sleep and food that isn't in a ration pack. And if anyone even thinks about putting me on bait duty again, I swear I'll throw them to the next Grave Titan myself."

Cal chuckled, but the thought of food made his stomach twist. It had been hours since he had eaten, and the exhaustion only made the hunger worse. He pulled a ration bar from his pack, the wrapper crinkling in the quiet space, and took a slow bite. It tasted like sawdust and salt.

Vanguard rations were efficient, not enjoyable.

Daryas watched him, then nodded toward the others. "Get some rest. We'll figure out our next move at first light."

Cal hesitated, then glanced between them. "You all fight like you've been doing this forever. How long have you been together?"

Daryas exchanged a glance with the others before smirking. "Long enough."

"We're the War Angels," Smokey said, stretching his arms over his head with a lazy smirk. "Best damn Vanguard squad in the coalition."

Cab let out a short snort. "According to us."

"The only opinions that matter," Grassie countered, propping her boots up on a supply crate. "Besides, we've lasted longer than most. That counts for something."

Cal leaned forward, arms resting on his knees. "War Angels… why that name?"

Daryas smirked. "Started as a joke. Our old commander used to say we hit like an airstrike from heaven—heavy, fast, and more than the enemy could handle." She exhaled through her nose. "Guess the name stuck."

Smokey chuckled. "Yeah, well, we've made it our own since then. Each of us brings something different to the team."

"Daryas is our hammer," Cab said, tapping a gloved fist against her knee. "Leads from the front, hits harder than anyone."

"Smokey's our sharp eye," Grassie added, stretching out her legs. "If he takes a shot, it lands."

Smokey clicked his tongue, flashing a lopsided grin. "Cab's the one who keeps us all breathing. If you go down, she's the one dragging your sorry ass back up—whether you want her to or not."

Cal arched a brow. "And Grassie?"

Grassie smirked, leaning back with a stretch. "I keep these dumbasses alive. Fastest on the field. Best at getting us out of bad situations—usually the ones *they* get us into."

Cal leaned back slightly, watching the way they spoke about each other—not just as teammates, but as something closer. Their words carried the weight of shared fights, scars, near-misses that no outsider could fully understand.

He'd seen them fight, but this was different. It wasn't just coordination—it was trust.

"And Rich?" he asked, looking around.

Daryas smirked. "Rich is Rich. He's the guy who makes sure we come back alive. He's saved our asses more times than I can count."

Cal nodded slowly. He wasn't just traveling with elite fighters—he was among legends in the making.

"So who do you report to?" he asked, glancing between them.

Daryas tilted her head slightly, considering the question. "Only Commander Varek. We don't answer to anyone else."

Cal frowned. "Not even the other commanders?"

Smokey chuckled. "They give orders sometimes, sure. But out here? Varek's word is final. That's all that matters. He's the top commander. Controls everything at our stronghold."

"Alright, enough talking," Daryas finally said, her voice carrying finality. "Get some sleep. We've got a long road ahead of us."

Cal leaned back, but his mind kept turning. The War Angels. He didn't know if he'd ever belong among them—but for now, he was grateful to be here.

Cal hesitated before asking, "What is the next move?"

She exhaled, running a hand through her hair. "We regroup with the convoy. If they made it past the stronghold, they should be setting up a new position somewhere ahead. That's where we need to be."

A lump settled in Cal's throat. He had spent all day focusing on moving, on surviving, and hadn't let himself think about what came next. The convoy meant returning to Varek. Less than a day ago, he'd been on an airship, and now he was here—worn out, sore, and carrying memories that felt heavier than his pack. It wasn't that he had changed, but he couldn't shake the feeling that everything around him had.

"Get some sleep, Miner," Daryas said, turning away. "Tomorrow's going to be a long day."

Cal nodded slowly, leaning his head back against the wall. He closed his eyes, willing himself to rest. But sleep wouldn't come easy—not when there were still so many questions left unanswered.

For the first time since this all began, he wasn't just a miner trying to survive.

And that scared him more than the undead ever had.

Sleep did not come easily. Cal's body was exhausted, but his mind refused to shut down. He shifted against the cold wall, listening to the soft breathing of the others, the occasional shifting of gear. It was strange to feel safe—even temporarily—after the night they'd had. His fingers absently traced the grip of his sidearm, a reminder of how quickly things could change.

Somewhere outside, something moved. A faint scraping sound. He tensed, holding his breath, but it faded just as quickly as it had come. A stray infected? The wind against debris? He couldn't be sure.

"You hear that too?" Smokey's voice was quiet, barely above a whisper.

Cal turned his head, finding the Vanguard sitting against the opposite wall, watching him. His rifle rested across his lap, but his posture was relaxed, like he had been waiting for something.

"Probably nothing," Cal murmured, not entirely convinced.

"Yeah, probably," Smokey agreed, but he kept his weapon close all the same.

A few beats of silence passed before Smokey spoke again. "You thinking about tomorrow?"

Cal exhaled slowly. "I don't know what I'm thinking about."

Smokey smirked. "Yeah. That tracks."

Cal let his head rest against the wall again. "What happens when we get back to the convoy?"

Grassie shrugged. "Varek will want answers. Corvin, too. But you're not just some lost miner anymore. You pulled our asses out of the fire, twice now. People are gonna hear about that. We'll make sure of it."

Cal didn't know how to feel about that. He had spent his whole life in the background, just another worker in the system. Now, for better or worse, so many people were paying attention.

"Try to sleep, Miner," Smokey said, shifting to get comfortable. "Tomorrow, you'll need it."

Cal nodded, though he wasn't sure he could. Too many questions, too many things left uncertain.

Still, as he closed his eyes, listening to the rhythmic breathing of those around him, he felt something he hadn't felt in a long time.

Something close to belonging.

The morning came too soon.

Cal stirred, feeling every ache and bruise as he sat up. The air inside the depot was stagnant, thick with dust and the lingering scent of rust and old fuel. The structure had held through the night, offering them the rare comfort of uninterrupted rest, but something about the silence felt wrong.

Daryas and Cab were already up, quietly checking their gear. Grassie sat against a crate, staring off into the dim interior, lost in thought. Smokey stretched, groaning as he adjusted his rifle strap. "Alright, what's the damage? Everyone still in one piece?"

"Physically? Sure," Cab muttered. "Mentally? I think we're all running on fumes."

Cal rubbed his eyes before glancing around. "We should check this place. See if there's anything useful before we move out."

Daryas nodded. "Good call. Keep it quiet, though. We don't know if we're alone."

They spread out, cautiously moving through the depot. Most of the supply crates had already been ransacked, their contents long gone, but a few remained sealed. Smokey pried one open with the butt of his knife, revealing a stash of emergency rations and a handful of medical supplies. "Jackpot," he said with a grin, tossing a ration pack to Cal. "Breakfast of champions."

Cal caught it, peeling it open and taking a bite. It was just as dry and flavorless as the last one, but hunger made it tolerable. As he chewed, his gaze wandered to the far end of the depot, where a reinforced steel door stood partially ajar.

Something about it felt... off.

"I'm checking that door," he said, gesturing toward it. Daryas followed as he approached, her rifle at the ready.

Cal pushed it open slowly, revealing a dark corridor leading deeper into the depot's lower levels. The air was colder here, and the scent of decay clung to the walls. He took a cautious step inside, his boots scraping against the dust-covered floor.

Then he saw it.

A terminal, still powered, its screen faintly glowing in the dim light.

Daryas frowned. "That shouldn't be working."

Cal stepped closer, scanning the interface. The text was fragmented, but parts of it were still readable.

"—Sector clearance initiated. All remaining personnel advised to evacuate before scheduled purge—"

Daryas stiffened. "We need to move. Now."

Before they could react, a distant rumble vibrated through the walls. Something was happening outside.

They rushed back to the others, who had already noticed the noise. "We've got movement," Cab reported, pointing toward the entrance. "A group passing through. Armed."

Cal's pulse quickened. They crept toward the barricade, peering through a narrow gap in the metal. A line of figures moved in the distance, methodical and deliberate. They weren't scavengers or stragglers. They were something else.

The voices carried faintly on the wind.

"...last group already moved ahead..."

"...need to clear the sector before the purge..."

"...won't take long, then we head to the next site."

Daryas exhaled slowly. "We need to get out of here before they notice us."

Cal watched as the group continued past, heading toward the ruins of the stronghold. The figures stopped near the site, scanning the destruction.

One of them muttered something into a radio.

Then, they moved on.

Cal let out a slow breath, feeling the weight of what they had just overheard settle over him like a heavy cloak. The Vanguard remained crouched behind their cover, unmoving, waiting until the last echoes of the group's footsteps disappeared into the distance.

Cal's mind raced, trying to piece it together. The wreckage of the stronghold, the Grave Titan being drawn in, the cryptic message on the terminal—it all pointed to something deliberate. But why?

Grassie shifted uncomfortably. "I don't like this. If they're planning something, we're right in the middle of it."

"Then we need to get out of the middle," Cab said. "Fast."

Daryas scanned the horizon. "We'll move out in five. Make sure you have everything you need. We don't stop until we're far from here."

The group moved quickly, gathering their supplies and double-checking their weapons. The air felt heavier now, charged with an unease none of them spoke aloud. Cal shouldered his pack that he had scavenged from the building they found themselves in, casting one last glance toward the stronghold's remains.

The figures had disappeared into the wasteland beyond, but their words lingered.

Something was coming.

And Cal had the sinking feeling that the undead weren't the worst thing out there.

Chapter 9 - Between Two Worlds

The journey back to the convoy was almost unnervingly easy.

After the chaos of the stronghold, the relentless fight for survival, Cal had expected more—more undead, more stragglers, more signs of destruction. Instead, the wasteland stretched before them in eerie silence, the wind stirring dust over cracked earth and rusted wreckage.

Daryas led the War Angels without a word, their movements precise, controlled—a formation as natural as breathing. Boots crushed dry earth in a rhythmic cadence, weapons scanning, ready, never truly at rest.

But as the wasteland stretched empty before them, even their rigid postures began to loosen, just slightly. The tension of the fight hadn't left, but survival no longer felt like a second-to-second gamble.

Every so often, Cal caught them exchanging glances, silent confirmations that their path remained clear. He had thought he might get used to traveling with them, but the precision with which they moved still felt like something from another world.

Something inside him had shifted, too. He didn't just follow anymore—he scanned the landscape as they did, tracking distant movement, searching for threats before they appeared. The convoy rose on the horizon, its towers and reinforced outposts cutting into the sky like a fortress of steel. A place that should have felt like safety. Like home.

But as they closed the distance, something knotted in Cal's chest. A hesitation he hadn't expected.

He had survived the stronghold. He had walked among the War Angels.

The Vanguard checkpoint came into view, a fortified position at the edge of the moving encampment. The convoy was still preparing for the crossing. The massive transports lined up in formation, ready to move at a moment's notice. Soldiers and workers moved in steady, coordinated effort, ensuring everything was secured for the dangerous trek ahead.

As if Cal had never fallen from an airship. As if he hadn't faced death alongside the War Angels.

The convoy's outer barricade loomed ahead, soldiers shifting as they caught sight of the approaching group. Weapons weren't raised, but hands tensed near holsters, eyes flickering between the War Angels and the boy walking with them.

The guards at the checkpoint exchanged uneasy glances. They knew the War Angels by reputation—and reputations carried weight.

Then Daryas stepped forward.

"We're back," she said simply.

That was all it took. The tension snapped like a wire pulled too tight, then released. A brief pause, then a curt nod from the lead guard.

"Let them through."

The War Angels had weight here, a presence that demanded respect. All the Vanguard were admired by the entire stronghold, but the Angels were clearly a step above. Cal could see it in the way soldiers straightened when they passed, in the murmurs of recognition trailing in their wake.

Then, just as they stepped beyond the barricades, a familiar voice rang out.

"Miner."

The voice cut through the low murmurs of the camp like a blade.

Cal turned.

Varek was already moving toward him, his posture unreadable, his gaze sharp as ever. The way soldiers instinctively cleared a path as he passed wasn't out of fear—it was the kind of presence that didn't need to demand space. It was simply given.

His uniform was crisp, his movements fluid but measured. He wasn't the kind of man who rushed, yet here he was, closing the distance with clear intent.

The War Angels peeled away, giving Cal space. They knew better than to linger when Varek wanted someone's attention.

"Walk with me," Varek said, already turning before Cal could respond.

Cal fell into step beside him, his heart hammering for reasons he didn't entirely understand. Behind him, the War Angels followed at a slight distance, their presence a silent but deliberate statement—they were here to give their report, but Varek had chosen to address Cal first.

The commander's pace was steady, but there was something in his stance that felt different. Not just the usual controlled authority, but something more—something heavier. Relief, maybe.

"When I saw you go over that rail, I thought we'd lost you," Varek admitted, his voice low enough that only Cal could hear. It wasn't an emotional statement, but there was weight to it.

He had been on that airship. He had watched Cal fall.

Yet here they were.

Varek didn't speak at first. He simply walked, hands clasped behind his back, his gaze sweeping over the convoy's operations.

Workers unloaded supply crates, engineers calibrated defense turrets, soldiers maintained their weapons. It was the seamless movement of an efficient machine, a system kept running by discipline, necessity, and a quiet, ever-present authority.

Finally, Varek exhaled through his nose, shaking his head slightly. "I sent the War Angels after you. They don't deploy for just anyone."

Cal frowned. "I figured as much. But why?"

Varek gave him a sidelong glance, something unreadable flickering in his expression. "Because I don't waste potential."

Cal felt the weight of those words settle over him, but before he could respond, Varek continued walking, his gaze fixed on the horizon.

"Tell me what happened," he said simply. Not an order, not an interrogation—just a quiet expectation.

Cal hesitated, then started from the beginning. The airship attack, the fall, waking up alone. Meeting the War Angels, fighting through the stronghold, the Grave Titan, everything. He kept his words measured, factual, but the weight of it all still pressed on his chest. He had lived through it, but saying it aloud made it feel more real.

Varek listened without interrupting, nodding occasionally but otherwise giving nothing away. When Cal finished, silence stretched between them.

Then Varek spoke. "You adapted. Most wouldn't have." He studied Cal, his gaze sharp. "And when you saw an opportunity, you took it. That's what makes a soldier. That's what makes a leader."

Cal opened his mouth, but Varek held up a hand. "Don't overthink it, Miner. You're not there yet. But you could be.

That's what makes you interesting. That's why I keep you around."

Cal swallowed hard, unsure if that was a promise or a warning.

Varek finally slowed his pace, stopping near the edge of the encampment. "Go clean up. Get some rest. We'll talk soon." He turned slightly, nodding toward the War Angels. "I have a debriefing to finish."

Just like that, Varek was gone, moving toward the War Angels without another word. Cal exhaled, feeling like he had just stepped into something far bigger than himself—something he wasn't sure he fully understood yet.

Varek left him standing there, the sounds of the convoy filling the space he had occupied. Cal exhaled, forcing himself to move again.

He wasn't sure what had just happened, but he felt as though something had shifted yet again.

Reuniting with his parents felt like stepping into a different life.

The moment he saw them, standing near one of the supply stations, he felt an unfamiliar knot tighten in his chest. They were alive, unharmed, their expressions shifting from exhaustion to relief the instant they spotted him.

His mother got to him first, her hands gripping his arms as she looked him over. "Cal—by the sky, you're okay."

His father stood a step behind, his face unreadable. But his shoulders, normally squared and firm, seemed to ease slightly.

"I'm fine," Cal said, though he wasn't entirely sure that was true.

His mother's grip didn't loosen. "We heard about the airship. They said you were lost. We thought—"

"I made it," Cal interrupted gently. "I made it back."

Joran appeared then, lingering just behind them, his usual sharp tongue momentarily absent. His expression was difficult to read—something between disbelief and something else. Something heavier.

Cal hesitated, then finally spoke. "There's... a lot to tell you."

They listened as he explained. He told them about the crash, about the War Angels, about the stronghold and the Grave Titan and everything in between. He kept his voice steady, though the memories still felt too fresh, too raw.

His father sat down on an overturned supply crate, rubbing his jaw as he processed it all. His mother held onto his arm a little too tightly, like she feared he might disappear again. Joran stood with his arms crossed, nodding along, but his eyes held something else—something between admiration and unease.

"So... you were fighting with the Vanguard?" Joran finally asked. "Like, actual combat?"

"Not exactly," Cal admitted. "I helped. I came up with a plan to get through the stronghold. They listened."

Joran let out a low whistle. "They listened... to *you?*"

Cal shrugged, feeling suddenly self-conscious. "The plan made sense."

His mother exhaled, shaking her head. "Cal, this is... a lot. You could have been killed."

"I know," he said quietly.

A heavy silence settled between them. Then Joran cleared his throat, trying to lighten the moment. "Well, if this whole mining thing doesn't work out, maybe you can start leading missions full-time."

Cal let out a small, tired chuckle. "There's a long way to go before that even becomes a possibility. You should have seen me try to handle the gun they gave me."

As he said it, a thought struck him. His pack felt heavier than it should have. He frowned, shifting it off his shoulder and opening the top flap. His fingers brushed against cold metal. The gun. He had forgotten he still had it. He hadn't even thought about it since leaving the storage depot where they slept the night before.

For a moment, he just stared at it. It was smaller than the Vanguard weapons but heavier than what he was used to. It didn't belong in a miner's hands, but here it was, his by circumstance.

Joran's parents stepped up to the group, their presence familiar and grounding. His father, a broad-shouldered man with the same sharp wit as his son, clapped a hand on Joran's shoulder. "Took you long enough to find him. We thought maybe he got too important for us back here."

His mother, her face lined with exhaustion from years in the mines, crossed her arms. "He always was a troublemaker. I half-expected him to come back in Vanguard armor already."

Joran rolled his eyes. "Oh, come on, Ma. Give it a few weeks."

Cal chuckled, shaking his head. "No chance of that."

Joran's father turned to Cal, his expression softening just a bit. "We're glad you're alright, kid. We've started hearing rumors. Can't believe half of them."

"Probably best if you don't," Cal muttered. "Most of it still doesn't feel real."

His father clapped his hands together, breaking the tension. "Alright. Enough heavy talk. We should eat. Get some real food before the next damn disaster hits."

His mother nodded. "Come. Sit with us, Cal. Just for a little while."

For the first time in what felt like forever, he did. The smell of cooked rations filled the air as they found a spot near one of the smaller fires. The warmth of the flames flickered against the metal hulls of supply crates, casting long shadows in the dimming light.

Conversation flowed in small, quiet moments. Joran's father launched into a familiar story about a mining collapse years back, one they had all heard before but still listened to as if it were the first time. His mother chimed in with details he exaggerated or conveniently forgot. "And don't forget," she added, "he spent half the day stuck in the rubble before anyone realized he wasn't just taking a nap."

Joran groaned. "You're going to tell that story forever, aren't you?"

"Absolutely," his father smirked.

Joran's father leaned forward, nudging Cal with an elbow. "I overheard a soldier talking about you earlier. Said you ran with the War Angels and took down a Grave Titan." He raised a brow. "That true, or is the rumor mill already getting creative?"

Cal exhaled, shaking his head. "Most of it is probably overblown. We fought through a ransacked stronghold, figured out a way to take down the Titan. That's all."

Joran let out a dramatic sigh. "Oh sure, just a Grave Titan. Just one of the biggest things to ever exist outside of nightmares."

"You're making it sound cooler than it was," Cal shot back.

Joran's father chuckled. "That's what stories are for, Cal. Making things sound bigger than life."

Cal let the words settle. Maybe that was true. Maybe this would all become legend one day, twisted in retelling until even he wouldn't recognize himself in the stories.

Joran's mother handed him another ration pack, nodding toward him. "You need to eat, Cal. Bet you haven't had a proper meal since all this started."

He hadn't thought about it, but she was probably right. He'd barely eaten since the crash. Just the sawdusty Vanguard field rations.

For the first time in the weeks since he had started observing the soldiers, he allowed himself to relax, to sink into the familiar rhythm of the convoy, the comfort of old stories, shared meals, and the warmth of people who, despite everything, still felt like home.

And for a moment, Cal let himself breathe. No War Angels, no Varek, no Grave Titans looming in his mind.

Just family. Just the convoy.

Just a moment of normal.

Chapter 10 – The Weight of Questions

The convoy moved like a living organism, a carefully choreographed machine grinding forward into the unknown.

The air was sharp with the crisp chill of higher elevation as they ascended the winding path toward the mountain pass. The terrain grew more treacherous, forcing the massive transports to slow as workers cleared debris, reinforced makeshift paths, and scouted ahead for any threats. There were remnants of old trails here, signs that other coalitions had passed through before, but time and the wasteland had nearly reclaimed them. Despite the dangers of travel, there was an almost unsettling calm. The undead were nowhere in sight. No sudden ambushes, no ominous shadows on the horizon. Just the slow, methodical movement of the convoy pushing toward the next stronghold site.

Cal stood beside Varek, high up on one of the mobile command platforms, watching it all unfold. He had expected tension, expected chaos, but instead, he found himself witnessing something strangely... controlled. Organized.

Varek must have noticed his expression. "You thought it would be more dramatic, didn't you?"

Cal hesitated before nodding. "I guess I did. It always felt dramatic, chaotic, when I was helping my family move. I guess the bigger picture makes all that just feel... small."

Varek gave a short, knowing hum. "Efficiency isn't exciting, Miner. It's just necessary."

They watched as squads of engineers and soldiers moved supplies, checked armor plating, and ran field diagnostics on the towering war machines stationed throughout the convoy. Everything had its place, its purpose. Varek, naturally, was at the center of it all, overseeing logistics, issuing commands, making sure every moving part did its job without hesitation.

"Every time we move," Varek continued, "it's a calculated risk. Resource management, defensive positioning, terrain assessments—all of it plays a role in ensuring we don't get caught off guard."

Cal frowned. "And if something goes wrong?"

Varek's lips quirked into something that wasn't quite a smile. "Then we improvise."

For the next few hours, Cal followed him through the convoy, watching how every piece of the operation connected. How supplies were allocated, how troops were rotated for rest, how reconnaissance teams moved ahead to ensure safe passage. It was an unspoken lesson—one Cal realized Varek had no intention of teaching in words. He was meant to observe, to learn through experience.

It made him wonder how much of this knowledge Varek had been handed when he was young. And how much he had to fight for himself.

At one point, as they paused near one of the supply transports, Cal finally voiced the thought that had been gnawing at him.

"Before we left the last stronghold, the place was wiped clean. Too clean. Like no one had even tried to hold it." Cal kept his voice measured, casual, but his stomach twisted as he watched Varek's reaction. "Why did we do that?"

Varek's expression remained neutral, but his eyes flicked toward Cal just slightly before turning back to the convoy. "You're asking a lot of questions lately, Miner."

Cal crossed his arms. "I thought that was what you wanted me to do. Observe. Learn. Figure things out."

Varek exhaled through his nose, his voice taking on a sharper edge. "There's a difference between learning and prying into things that don't concern you."

The words hit harder than Cal expected. He clenched his jaw but held his ground. "It does concern me. When we started leaving the old stronghold, everything was wiped clean—fires doused, tracks erased, even the signs that we had ever lived there. Like we were never meant to exist in that place. Then back at the stronghold that had already fallen, I overheard survivors mention something about a 'purge.' I don't know what they meant, but the way they said it... it was like they knew something was coming. Like it was going to erase the ruins. Are they connected?"

Varek stopped walking, turning fully to face him. The air between them felt heavier now, charged with something unspoken. For a long moment, Varek said nothing. Then, just when Cal was starting to think he had truly overstepped, Varek's shoulders loosened slightly. He ran a hand down his face and let out a quiet chuckle—one that didn't reach his eyes.

"You remind me of someone," Varek said at last, his voice softer but no less weighted. "Too stubborn for his own good. Too eager to see a grand conspiracy in every shadow."

Cal didn't look away. "And were they wrong?"

Varek's jaw tightened slightly before he let out a slow breath. "If they weren't, it doesn't change anything for us. We move forward, we secure the next position, and we make sure we don't end up like them."

Something about the way he said it made Cal's stomach twist. Varek didn't wait for a response before he started walking again, his tone shifting back to something calmer, more controlled. "We live in a world of inevitabilities, Miner. People disappear. Strongholds fall. It isn't about why—it's about what you do next. That's the only thing that matters."

Cal wasn't satisfied. "And the way we left our own stronghold? The way we erased everything before moving out—why? What does that have to do with survival?"

Varek's jaw tightened, but when he answered, his tone was smoother. More prepared. "Because if we don't, we invite trouble. The infected don't think, but they react. If they find signs of recent life, they linger, waiting for it to return. If another group stumbles upon our traces, they might follow. We don't need the kind of attention that invites."

He turned his gaze back to the moving convoy. "Clean ground means a fresh start. We take only what we need and leave nothing that can be used against us."

Cal stared at him, unsatisfied. "But the ones that overran the last stronghold? The survivors talked about something—like they knew something was coming. If this is just about covering our tracks, why did they mention a 'purge'?"

Varek exhaled through his nose, his tone measured. "People in a losing fight say a lot of things. Desperation makes them see patterns where there aren't any. Maybe they were just trying to justify that coalition's failure. Maybe 'purge' was their word for losing control of the stronghold."

Cal frowned, watching him closely. "It didn't sound like they were talking about something that had already happened. It was like they were waiting for it. Expecting it. They weren't just scared of the past—they were afraid of what was coming next."

"Does it matter?" Varek's voice hardened just slightly, and for the first time, his gaze met Cal's fully, pinning him in place. "What matters is keeping the people in this convoy alive. You want to ask questions? Ask about supply chains. Ask about defense lines. Ask about something that actually keeps us moving."

Cal clenched his jaw, forcing himself to nod. He could push no further.

Varek's jaw twitched. "I'm telling you that thinking too hard about things beyond your station will get you nowhere." His voice had sharpened again, irritation slipping through. "We all have roles to play. If you want to be useful, then learn how things work. Learn how to keep people alive."

Cal held his gaze. "And if there's something bigger at play?"

Varek exhaled slowly, looking past him, past the convoy, toward the mountains ahead. "Then that's not your problem."

Cal decided to let the matter drop, he could tell he had pushed further than Varek wanted, but something about the way Varek answered him—his carefully neutral tone, the way he didn't quite meet Cal's eyes until pressed—made the explanation feel hollow.

Cal frowned but didn't press further. He could tell Varek wanted this conversation buried, that every answer had been designed to guide him away rather than satisfy his curiosity. The way he spoke, the subtle shifts in his tone—there was something just beneath the surface, something Varek didn't want him to see.

Cal forced himself to nod, as if accepting the explanation, but deep down, he knew this wasn't over. Varek knew something. And one way or another, Cal would figure out what it was.

Before he could press further, Corvin appeared, approaching with an air of comfortable authority. His long coat swayed slightly in the cold wind, and as always, that briefcase was secured to his wrist.

"Commander," Corvin greeted smoothly. His gaze flicked briefly to Cal, then back to Varek. "We should discuss the next phase of operations."

Varek nodded. "Walk with us."

Cal fell into step beside them, his attention briefly flicking to Corvin's case. He had seen a glimpse of what was inside before— something metallic, something that had clearly meant something important. And yet, no one had spoken about it since.

"What's in the case?" Cal asked bluntly.

Corvin didn't even break stride. "Classified."

Cal shot him a look. "Everything's classified today."

Varek let out a low chuckle at that, but Corvin's expression remained unreadable. "Some knowledge is a burden, Miner. Be careful what you ask for."

Cal clenched his fists but forced himself to keep his expression neutral. He knew when a door was closed. For now, he let the silence stretch between them as they walked, following Varek and Corvin through the center of the convoy.

The mountain pass loomed ahead, the jagged cliffs casting long shadows over the winding trail. The convoy was making steady progress, but the ascent was slow—vehicles struggled against the thinning air, and the troops rotated in shifts to scout ahead, ensuring no unexpected threats waited for them.

Cal had expected more resistance, but so far, the journey had been eerily quiet. He glanced toward Varek. "The infected don't come this high?"

"They do," Varek replied. "But not often. The cold slows them. Makes them easier to deal with when they do show up." His eyes scanned the ridgeline. "That said, the pass isn't safe. We're still exposed here."

Cal followed his gaze. There was too much open space, too many places for an ambush to come from. He hated not knowing what was waiting for them ahead.

They continued in silence for a while, the sounds of the convoy filling the space—engines rumbling, boots crunching against loose gravel, the occasional barked order as supplies were shifted between vehicles. It was almost hypnotic, the routine of it all.

Then, out of the corner of his eye, Cal noticed Corvin adjusting his grip on the briefcase.

Something about the movement struck him as deliberate. Protective.

He decided to press his luck.

"So," Cal said, forcing his voice into something casual. "You always carry that thing around, or is today special?"

Corvin barely reacted, his stride unwavering. "It's always with me."

"Must be important."

Corvin smiled, but there was no warmth in it. "Everything I deal with is important."

Cal tilted his head slightly, pushing just a little more. "Important enough to be chained to your wrist?"

Corvin let out a quiet breath—something that might have been amusement, but it was impossible to tell. "Necessary."

Varek finally glanced at him, his expression unreadable. "Curiosity can be dangerous, Miner."

Cal met his gaze, holding it for just a moment too long before shrugging. "So I've been told."

For the first time, Corvin actually looked at him, studying him in a way that made Cal feel like he was being dissected. Finally, the man gave a short nod and turned his attention forward again. "Let's focus on what actually matters."

The way he said it sent another chill through Cal's spine.

The next few days passed in a haze of routine. The convoy continued its climb, navigating the thinning paths of the pass, until they finally reached the other side. The descent was easier, but not without its challenges—the terrain was rough, and the vehicles had to move slowly to avoid sliding out of control.

It was on the second day of the descent that the first reports came in.

"Infected sighted," a scout relayed through the command channel. "Single stragglers at first. Now seeing more."

Cal stood with Varek and a group of officers at one of the forward stations, watching the reports come in. The vanguard teams had already moved out, positioning themselves at key chokepoints along the path, preparing for what could be an incoming horde.

"They're moving toward us," one of the officers noted, adjusting his rifle. "Something's drawing them."

Varek frowned. "How many?"

The scout's voice crackled through the comms. "Too soon to tell. Could be wanderers… or something worse."

The convoy wouldn't stop moving, but now the tension was palpable. Soldiers tightened their grips on weapons. Orders were issued to fortify weak points. The engineers worked faster, reinforcing supply vehicles in case they had to push through an attack.

For the first time in days, Cal felt it again.

That weight in the air.

That certainty that something was coming.

And this time, he was going to see it unfold firsthand.

Chapter 11 – When the dead rise

The first sign of trouble was the shift in the wind.

Cal stood beside Varek on an elevated section of the barricade, watching as the first groups of infected approached. They were slow, shambling, nothing out of the ordinary. The soldiers along the perimeter readied their weapons, falling into well-practiced formations. There was no panic, no hesitation—just another engagement in the never-ending war against the dead.

"East wall is thinning," Cal noted, watching as a cluster of infected moved toward a section with fewer defenders. "They're pushing there harder."

Varek gave a curt nod and turned to a nearby officer. "Send a fire team to reinforce the east. Keep the line stable."

The officer relayed the order, and within moments, additional troops moved into position, raising their rifles and sending bursts of fire into the approaching horde. The infected dropped in waves, but more pressed forward to take their place. The pattern was familiar, manageable.

Cal scanned the field again. "There's a break in the north sector," he pointed out. "If we push from the west, we can funnel them into a kill zone."

Varek glanced at him, then back at the field. "Not bad." He gestured to another officer. "Deploy a strike team. Box them in."

The fight carried on, structured and tactical. The coalition had fought battles like this a thousand times before. Further down the line, the distinct hum of trexium-charged rifles cut through the chaos, bright pink streaks of energy slicing through the horde with deadly precision. Cal turned his head, catching glimpses of the War Angels carving a path through the infected, their movements coordinated, almost surgical. Daryas moved with sharp efficiency, her energy rifle firing in calculated bursts, while

Smokey perched high on a transport, lining up clean headshots that dropped targets in rapid succession. Rich tanked hits that would've staggered anyone else, his heavy frame absorbing the impact as he laid down suppressive fire. Grassie darted between cover, small and nimble, clearing out pockets of infected before they could overwhelm the soldiers. Cab, always watching for wounded, hauled a fallen trooper back behind the lines without missing a step.

Further down the battlefield, another vanguard team was in motion. Cal recognized the name—Bandit. He had heard the War Angels mention him before, a Vanguard leader known for his unpredictability. His team, the Time Bandits, moved with ruthless efficiency and speed—Nac, a wiry man with quick reflexes, darted between cover, his rifle sending bursts of pink energy into the crowd. Sib, more methodical, fired precise shots, always aiming for maximum damage. Fafa, a silent but unshakable presence, held the line with a heavy repeater, mowing down anything that came too close. And then there was Jmeli—her armor marked with a single, bold footprint across the chest plate. Even in the heat of combat, she found time to stomp a boot onto a fallen infected chest before blasting its head apart, grinning through the visor.

Beyond them, another Vanguard squad he hadn't seen before waded into the fray. More pink energy fire lit up the battlefield as they pushed back the growing tide. For a moment, it almost seemed like the coalition had the upper hand.

Then something changed.

The wind shifted again.

The first wet thud echoed across the battlefield.

The perimeter broke.

Cal stood near one of the barricades, watching the soldiers adjust their formations as the convoy settled into its temporary encampment. They had just begun fortifying the area when the first gunfire rang out in the distance. It wasn't unusual—skirmishes with stragglers were common when setting up a new position—but the intensity of the shots made his stomach twist. This wasn't just a routine cleanup.

Then the screams started.

Cal turned sharply toward the source of the commotion, catching sight of soldiers running toward the outer perimeter. From his vantage point, he could just make out the dark figures moving in the distance, stumbling and lurching in that telltale way. But something was different. They weren't just charging. They were throwing something.

A wet, sickening splat echoed through the air, followed by another. Then another. Small, misshapen lumps of flesh arced through the sky, landing among the defenders with dull thuds.

A beat of silence.

A soldier near the barricade, a younger recruit, took an uneasy step forward. The thing that had landed at his feet wasn't a grenade, wasn't a weapon he'd ever seen before. It was organic, pulsing slightly, like a bloated organ torn from some monstrous body. Its flesh was a mottled gray, veins of dark purple stretching along its surface, twitching as if still alive.

"What the hell is that?" another soldier muttered.

The recruit bent down slightly, his rifle shifting on his shoulder. "I think it's—"

Then it ruptured.

A sickening pop, like flesh splitting open under pressure. A dense, wet mist exploded outward, thick and heavy, carrying the sharp, rancid scent of decay. The recruit barely had time to stagger backward before the mist consumed him, clinging to his skin, sinking into his lungs with his next panicked breath.

He gasped.

Then he screamed.

At first, it seemed like he was just suffocating. His hands clawed at his throat, his body convulsing in violent spasms. Then, just as suddenly, he collapsed. His body twitched once, then went still.

Silence settled uneasily over the battlefield. More soldiers fell where they stood, choked by the mist, their bodies writhing before going still. The infected weren't attacking them. They were watching. Waiting.

Then, one by one, the bodies stirred.

The fallen soldiers pushed themselves up, their movements jerky and unnatural. Some let out a low, guttural growl as their fingers flexed, now curled into claw-like shapes. Their heads twitched in random directions before snapping forward, eyes now cloudy and vacant.

Then they turned on their former comrades.

Screams erupted anew as the freshly turned lunged at the living, catching them off guard in the chaos. Soldiers who had moved in to recover their dead were now within arm's reach of the infected, giving them no time to react before they were torn apart or bitten. What had been an orderly battle turned into a bloodbath in seconds.

"Fall back! Get away from the bodies!" someone shouted, but it was too late. The perimeter was already collapsing.

Panic erupted. Orders were shouted, but it was already too late—chaos had taken hold. The soldiers who weren't infected opened fire, but for every zombie they cut down, another took its place. And then the first of the newly infected staggered upright, twisted remnants of the very people who had been defending the stronghold only moments before.

Cal gritted his teeth. He needed to move. Needed to do something. His mind raced, analyzing the battlefield, searching for a solution. His eyes darted between pockets of resistance and weak points where the infected were pushing through.

"They're breaking through on the western perimeter," Cal said, voice steady despite the chaos. "If we concentrate fire along the ridge, we can force them into the bottleneck by the supply carriers. That'll give us time to reinforce the gaps."

Varek glanced at him, then back at the battlefield. "You think you can manage it?"

Cal hesitated, then nodded. "Yeah."

Varek didn't break stride. "Then get to it. Take command of the War Angels and execute the plan."

Cal's stomach twisted, but he turned, running toward the squad. The War Angels were already holding their ground, cutting down infected with ruthless efficiency. He reached them just as another explosion rocked the field. "Daryas! Shift your fire toward the ridge! We're forcing them into the bottleneck!"

Daryas barely glanced at him before nodding. "You heard him! Move!"

The team adjusted with practiced precision, repositioning as Smokey covered them from above. The plan was working—the infected were being funneled into a kill zone, their numbers momentarily stalled.

Then Cal's gaze snapped toward the other side of the convoy—toward where his parents were stationed.

And his stomach dropped.

Their section of the convoy was under attack. Not just from the infected, but from the virus bombs. He saw the dull pink mist lingering in the air, the panicked movements of people trying to flee. And in the center of it all—his mother. His father.

Staggering, coughing, clawing at the air as they struggled against the inevitable.

"No," he breathed, his pulse roaring in his ears. His legs moved before his mind could catch up, carrying him across the encampment as fast as they could.

"Cal! Hold your position!" Varek's voice cut through the chaos, sharp and commanding. "That's an order!"

Cal ignored him.

He barely noticed the shots ringing out around him, barely heard the shouts of warning. His eyes were locked on them.

They saw him coming. His mother reached out, her fingers trembling. His father fell to one knee, choking on something black and viscous.

Cal skidded to a halt just outside the worst of the mist, breathing heavily. "I'm here! I'm here, just—just hold on!"

His mother tried to speak, but her words came out broken, distorted by the infection tearing through her. Barely able to lift his head, his father was usually the stronger one. Pale and sweat-soaked, his face was changing; the veins darkened beneath the skin.

Cal's breath came in ragged gasps. He reached for them, but hesitated. His fingers curled into fists. He knew. He already knew.

His mother managed to whisper something, her voice barely a breath. He stepped closer, leaning in, desperate to hold onto the sound of her words before they were lost forever.

"Cal…" her voice was hoarse, but there was no fear in it— only love, only the warmth of a mother's voice comforting her child. "You have to go. You have to live."

"No," he said, shaking his head. "No, I can—"

His mother, her voice weak but steady, reached for him. "You have to go, Cal. You have to live. Don't look back."

His father swallowed hard, his body shuddering. "Promise us. No matter what happens. Keep going."

Cal clenched his jaw. He felt the weight of the gun that the War Angels had given him just a few days before in his holster. His fingers twitched toward it.

He knew what he had to do.

But he couldn't.

His vision blurred as his grip tightened on the weapon, his breath shuddering as he tried to steady himself. His parents were barely holding on, their bodies failing them as the infection took hold. He could see it in their eyes. The moment they lost themselves was coming.

Tears burned at the edges of his vision. He raised the gun.

His father's lips parted, as if to say something else—but his breath left him in a final, quiet sigh. His mother's fingers, still reaching toward him, fell limp in the dirt. The warmth in their faces faded, their expressions soft, peaceful, even as life slipped away. Too still. His mother collapsed beside him, her body limp, her chest rising and falling in shallow, uneven breaths that grew fainter with each passing second. A horrible, suffocating silence wrapped around them, and for the first time in Cal's life, his parents were unreachable.

His breath came in ragged, uneven gasps as he fell to his knees between them. His hands trembled as he reached out, his fingers ghosting over his mother's wrist, pressing lightly against skin that had already begun to cool. He waited—prayed—for the weak thump of a pulse.

Nothing.

As he turned towards his father, his vision was blurry. His strong, unshakable father, who had always told him to keep his head down, to work hard, to survive. Twisted and half-curled in the dirt, his body lay there; his slack face was deeply, profoundly wrong.

Cal inhaled sharply, a raw sound that barely passed as breathing. "Dad? Mom?" He was begging now, not just for their survival but for their presence—to hear his father tell him to be strong, to hear his mother remind him to be careful, just one more time. His hands shook violently as he reached toward them, but there was no response. No warmth. No recognition. No goodbye.

Only silence. The color drained from their skin, their limbs slack, as if whatever had been inside them had simply... shut down.

Cal's breath hitched. He crouched beside them, reaching out hesitantly, his fingers hovering over his mother's wrist. It was cold. Too cold.

For a long, agonizing moment, the world stopped. The battle, the screaming, the chaos—it all faded into a deafening, hollow void. All he could hear was the sound of his own breathing, sharp and uneven, like he was drowning in air.

Then something shifted.

A single, unnatural jerk of his father's fingers. A small, nearly imperceptible shudder through his mother's shoulders. Cal's breath hitched, his grief momentarily drowned by a sharp stab of dread.

No.

His stomach twisted as another convulsion rolled through them, their limbs twitching in erratic spasms. The veins on their arms darkened, thick and swollen beneath their skin, pulsating as if something beneath was moving, growing, changing.

A strangled noise caught in Cal's throat. He scrambled backward, his pulse a wild, frantic drumbeat against his ribs.

Please, no.

His father's fingers spasmed. A shudder ran through his mother's shoulders. Their limbs jerked once, then again, convulsions rippling through their still forms as something beneath the skin twisted, coiling, changing.

Cal scrambled backward, his pulse hammering. He wasn't ready. He wasn't ready for this.

Then their eyes snapped open—clouded, lifeless.

"Mom... Dad..." Cal's voice broke. His finger hovered over the trigger, shaking.

He couldn't do it.

He took a step back. Then another.

And then they moved.

Not as his parents. Not as the people who had raised him, who had taught him everything he knew.

As something else.

A choked sound tore from his throat as he stumbled backward, hands still shaking around the weapon. His breath came in ragged gasps, his body locked in place as the figures that had once been his parents turned toward him, their heads twitching unnaturally. They took a step forward, then another— faster now, the hesitation of their former selves burned away in the haze of infection.

Cal's grip tightened.

He had to do it. Had to pull the trigger.

But he couldn't.

A gunshot rang out.

Then another.

Cal flinched as both bodies jerked back violently, collapsing into the dirt with dull, final thuds.

His breath caught in his throat as he turned sharply, instinctively raising his own weapon.

Varek stood a few paces away, lowering his smoking pistol. His face was unreadable, his stance firm. He had been watching.

For a long moment, neither of them spoke. Cal's hands were still trembling, his breath still uneven.

Then Varek holstered his weapon and took a slow step forward. "Come on," he said, voice quieter than usual. "We need to move."

Cal swallowed hard, his throat tight. He looked down one last time.

Then, finally, he turned away.

Chapter 12 – What's left behind

The world had ended before, but never for Cal like this.

The battlefield was still alight with gunfire, the crack of rifles and the hum of trexium energy weapons filling the air. But to Cal, everything was muted, distant, like he was underwater. The taste of ash and blood coated his tongue, but he couldn't bring himself to move. His body felt leaden, his mind hollow.

His parents were gone.

He didn't know how long he stood there, staring at the bodies that no longer belonged to them. Their blood pooled dark in the dirt, already sinking into the earth, already fading from the world. It was as if they had never existed at all.

A hand landed on his shoulder.

Cal spun, his grief and rage igniting into something reckless. His fist was already swinging before he could think—before he could stop himself.

Varek caught it with ease.

With a sharp twist, he wrenched Cal's arm behind his back, pinning him in place in a single fluid motion. The movement was effortless, practiced, and Cal was suddenly reminded of just how far beneath Varek he was in skill and experience.

"If you want to take a swing at me," Varek said coolly, his grip firm but not cruel, "you better be able to make it land."

Cal gritted his teeth, struggling against the hold, but Varek didn't budge. His strength was a wall, unshakable, immovable. The fight drained from Cal's limbs almost as quickly as it had surged, leaving only exhaustion in its wake.

"You're not a soldier yet, boy," Varek continued, his tone edged with something almost like disappointment. "What makes you think you can take me on?"

Cal didn't have an answer. His breath came in ragged gasps, his body shaking with a mix of frustration and sorrow. He wanted to fight, wanted to lash out, but what was the point?

After a moment, Varek released him, stepping back. Cal staggered but stayed on his feet, his fists still clenched at his sides.

Cal flinched, turning sharply, his fingers instinctively tightening around his gun. Varek stood beside him, eyes heavy with something unreadable. Not pity. Not regret. Just a quiet understanding that made Cal's stomach turn.

"You should have listened," Varek said, his voice low, steady.

Cal's breath came sharply. A surge of emotion rose in his chest, something hot and painful, like fire licking up his throat. His arms trembled. His grip on the weapon turned his knuckles white. He thought about raising it, about pressing it against the chest of the man who had just gunned down his parents in front of him.

But he didn't.

Instead, his rage collapsed into something heavier. He turned away, exhaling a shuddering breath. "You didn't have to shoot them," he muttered, barely above a whisper.

Varek was quiet for a long moment. Then: "Yes, I did."

Cal shut his eyes. He didn't want to hear that. He didn't want to accept that Varek was right. Because if he did, then it meant there had never been another option.

And he needed to believe there had been another way.

"They were already gone, Cal." Varek's voice softened, but there was an edge of finality to it. "You know that."

Cal swallowed hard, his throat raw. He couldn't argue—not really. But the grief clawing at his insides refused to be silenced so easily.

A commotion near the medical tents pulled him back to reality.

Daryas was helping a wounded soldier onto a stretcher, her helmet discarded, strands of black hair falling loose from where it had been tied back. Smokey stood beside her, his usual smirk absent, his expression tight. Rich sat on the edge of another cot, his armor scuffed, his arm bound in a makeshift sling.

The War Angels.

Cal's stomach twisted as realization dawned. He had abandoned them. Left them without support. And now, Smokey was hurt because of it.

A sharp pang of guilt cut through the haze of his grief. He forced himself to move, his legs stiff as he crossed the camp. As he neared, Daryas glanced up, her dark eyes locking onto his.

"You made it," she said simply, but there was a weight in her voice that made his chest tighten.

Cal nodded, unable to speak past the lump in his throat. He looked at Smokey. "How bad?"

Rich gave a brief glance toward Smokey. "Doc says he'll live, but it was close. One of those runners almost got him before we pulled him out." Smokey shrugged but winced slightly at the movement.

Smokey let out a quiet scoff, but his eyes didn't hold their usual amusement. "Yeah, well, next time, maybe don't run off and leave us to die." His voice was flat, his anger quiet but sharp. "Dying in a real fight? Fine. Dying because someone didn't do their damn job? That's different."

Cal forced a breath through his nose. "It's my fault. I was distracted. I left you guys without oversight. I'm sorry."

The words felt heavy in his mouth, but he needed to say them. He had left his post. He had put them in danger. He had failed them.

Daryas studied him for a moment, then her expression hardened. "You think that makes it okay?"

"That's not the point." Cal clenched his fists. "You should have had someone watching your back."

Daryas took a step closer, her voice low but sharp. "Yeah we should have. And Smokey sure as hell shouldn't have had to pay the price for your distraction." She glanced at Smokey, her jaw tightening. "You left us out there, Cal. We needed you, and you ran. You don't get to just come back and act like a damn martyr. You don't get to say 'It's my fault' and think that makes it better."

There was another silence, but this time, it wasn't suffocating. It was understanding.

Daryas nodded toward the empty space beside Rich. "Sit down before you fall over."

Cal hesitated, then sank onto the edge of a supply crate. His muscles ached, his body finally catching up to the emotional toll of the last few hours. He was drained. Hollow. But something inside him burned—something steady, something unrelenting.

Varek had been right. He had been weak. He had let emotion dictate his actions, and because of that, people had gotten hurt.

That wasn't going to happen again.

He exhaled, straightening his shoulders. "I need to be better."

Daryas arched a brow. "Better?"

"I need to train. Fight. Learn everything I can." He swallowed, the edges of his grief sharpening into something solid. "I won't be weak again."

Smokey narrowed his eyes slightly, his usual smirk absent. "That so?"

Cal met his gaze, steady and unwavering. "Yeah."

For the first time since the battle, something like amusement flickered through the War Angels. Daryas exchanged a glance with Rich, then let out a quiet chuckle. "Well," she mused, leaning back, "guess we'll see what you're made of."

From across the camp, Varek watched, saying nothing.

The convoy traveled for days before they found their next stronghold location—a jagged cliffside that loomed over the valley below, offering a natural barrier on one side. It was the best defensive position they could have hoped for, forcing any attackers to approach from one of three fortified fronts instead of surrounding them completely.

Engineers and soldiers worked tirelessly to set up barriers, reinforce structures, and prepare for the long haul. The virus bombs had changed everything. They couldn't afford to just react anymore. They needed countermeasures. Scientists worked around the clock, testing protective gear and seeking ways to slow the infection before it could spread. The medical tents were still overwhelmed—those lucky enough to survive exposure to the mist were barely clinging to life.

Cal took stock of their numbers, the painful truth pressing in on him. The convoy had lost dozens in the last attack. He hadn't been counting before, but he was now. And he didn't like the math.

It took nearly a week for the stronghold to stabilize. Enough time for walls to go up, for supply chains to be reestablished.

Enough time for people to realize how much emptier the camp felt.

One evening, as the sun dipped low behind the mountains, Cal found himself near the worker's quarter, scanning the familiar faces. Relief flooded through him as he spotted Joran and his parents near one of the food stations. They looked exhausted, covered in dust from the journey, but they were alive.

Joran caught sight of him and waved him over. "You finally back from saving the world?"

Cal managed a small smile, but it felt hollow. "Something like that. You guys okay?"

Joran's mother gave him a tired but grateful nod. "We made it through, thanks to the Vanguard holding the line. But things feel different now. People are scared."

Joran's father crossed his arms, his expression unreadable. "They say the scientists are working on something. Some kind of treatment. But no one's saying how close they are."

Cal nodded, glancing toward the center of camp where the research teams were holed up. "They'll figure it out. They have to."

Joran frowned, stepping closer. "And you? How are you holding up?"

Cal opened his mouth to answer, but nothing came out. His throat felt tight. Joran was his best friend—he should be able to say something, anything, but the words just wouldn't come.

Joran sighed and shook his head. "You don't have to say it. I know."

His mother reached out, squeezing Cal's shoulder gently. "We're just glad you made it back. When we heard what happened, we feared the worst."

Joran's father exhaled, rubbing the back of his neck. "Your parents were good people, Cal. They were proud of you."

Cal swallowed hard, nodding, but he couldn't bring himself to look at them. The grief sat heavy in his chest, too raw to unpack. Instead, he forced a breath and tried to push through it.

Joran nudged him lightly. "You're not alone, you know. You don't have to go through this alone."

Cal gave a weak smirk. "Yeah? Feels like it."

Joran scoffed. "Please. You think I'd let you go all tragic loner on me? Not a chance."

Cal chuckled, the first genuine laugh he'd had in days. It was brief, but for a moment, the weight eased just a little. Joran grinned, satisfied. "Come find me later, alright? We'll talk. Or not. Whatever you need."

Cal nodded. "Yeah. I will."

Joran clapped a hand on his shoulder, then stepped back with his parents, giving him space. But as they walked away, Cal knew they weren't really leaving him behind.

Joran studied him for a moment before lowering his voice. "And you? What now?"

Cal exhaled, feeling the weight of everything settling onto his shoulders. "Now? I train. I learn. I make sure this never happens again."

Joran gave him a long look before nodding. "Then I guess I'll see you around."

Cal watched him go, the familiar ache in his chest pressing deeper. The past few days had changed everything, torn apart what little sense of stability he had left. But as Joran walked away, there was no distance between them, no uncertainty in his step. Just trust. Just understanding.

He let out a slow breath and turned back toward the camp, his mind already shifting to what came next. There was no time to waste. He had work to do.

Chapter 13 – Strength and Knowledge

Cal spent more time at the drill grounds than anywhere else. The air was thick with sweat and exertion, the rhythmic clang of metal on metal ringing through the open space as soldiers sparred, drilled formations, and honed their technique. At first, he remained an outsider, lingering at the edges, watching, studying every movement. He memorized the way the Vanguard moved, how their stances were always balanced, their weight perfectly distributed for speed and power. The way they anticipated attacks before they came, reacting with precision honed through relentless repetition.

He watched as recruits, barely more experienced than he was, took beatings and got back up, as instructors barked orders without the slightest ounce of patience. He saw men and women collapse from exhaustion, only to be hauled back to their feet by the same people who had just knocked them down. It was brutal. Unforgiving. But it was shaping them into something more than just survivors.

But watching wasn't enough anymore. The need to stand on the sidelines faded, replaced by something heavier. Something undeniable. Every second he spent observing, he felt the weight of inaction press down on him. It wasn't just about learning anymore. It was about becoming. If he wasn't fighting, if he wasn't pushing forward, then what had all of this suffering been for? At first, he lingered at the edges, watching, studying. He memorized the way the Vanguard moved, the efficiency in their strikes, the precision in their formations. But watching wasn't enough anymore.

The shift happened the moment his parents died.

In the chaos of the battle, in the days after, he had still been an observer—watching, listening, absorbing. But something had changed inside him. It wasn't just about survival anymore. The idea of standing on the sidelines felt unbearable. He wasn't a soldier yet, wasn't trained like the Vanguard, but the weight of inaction felt worse than any fight ever could.

He wanted to be in the fight, not just watching from the edges. He wanted to move, to strike, to be more than just an observer in a world that only rewarded those who took action. Because if he wasn't fighting, if he wasn't pushing forward, then what had all of this suffering been for?

One evening, as the sun bled into the horizon, Cal approached the training grounds with more than just intent to watch. Varek was there, as always, his presence a silent pillar at the heart of every drill.

Cal swallowed hard, then stepped forward. "I want in."

Varek turned, his gaze assessing. "Do you?"

Cal nodded, his pulse pounding in his ears. "I'm done watching. I want to fight."

For a long moment, Varek said nothing. Then he exhaled through his nose, nodding slightly. "Do you know what this means? What this life takes from you? What it will make you?"

Cal hesitated. He had thought about this—endlessly. Since the moment his parents died, since the War Angels had barely made it out because of his mistake, since the convoy had nearly been wiped from existence. He had nothing left tying him to the past. No obligations. No expectations to stay in the mines. For the first time in his life, he was free to make this choice.

And that made him feel like hell.

He shouldn't feel free. He shouldn't feel like he had gained something from their deaths.

Varek must have seen the conflict in his expression because his voice softened, just a fraction. "This life isn't an escape, Miner. It's a commitment. You don't do it because there's nothing left for you—you do it because you know exactly what you're walking into. This is more than studying supply lines and drawing conclusions from scattered information."

Cal's fists clenched. He met Varek's gaze. "I know what I'm walking into. And I still want in."

Varek studied him for another long moment, then gave a short nod. "Then report to the training grounds at dawn. You're good at taking in information. But tomorrow we'll see if you're more than a miner who snuck his way where he doesn't belong."

The first morning, he reported to the training grounds early, the suns rays teasing in the distance. The anticipation burned in his veins. For weeks, he had been on the outskirts of battle, making plans, offering ideas. But now? Now, he was going to shape himself into something that could execute them. The camp was still waking, the fires from the night still smoldering, but Varek was already there, waiting.

"You're late," Varek said, though the sun had barely begun to crest the horizon.

Cal fell in line without argument. His body was still healing, the grief still fresh, but none of it mattered anymore. He would not be weak again.

His training began with the basics. He learned the mechanics of a rifle, how to clean it, how to strip it apart and put it back together blindfolded. How to control his breathing, to fire with precision, to conserve ammunition. Every shot counted. Every move had to be efficient. There was no wasted motion, no hesitation.

Hand-to-hand combat followed. Bruises and exhaustion defined his first week. The training was relentless—hours spent drilling the same motions over and over again until they became reflex. The first time Cal got a punch in on Varek, it barely landed, a glancing blow off his side. Varek swiftly turned him over, a boot gently pressing against his chest the very next second.

"You're learning," Varek admitted, stepping back. "But you're still too predictable."

Cal gritted his teeth, shoving himself up again. "Then teach me to be unpredictable."

Varek smirked, as if that was exactly what he had been waiting for. Varek sparred with him personally, demonstrating over and over again just how little Cal knew. Every time Cal rushed, he found himself on his back. Every time he hesitated, he found himself pinned.

"You're thinking too much," Varek muttered, stepping back after throwing him to the ground for what felt like the hundredth time. "Instincts will keep you alive. Thinking will get you killed."

Cal growled, pushing himself back to his feet, wiping blood from his lip. "Thinking got us through the stronghold."

Varek smirked, stepping back into position. "True. Then I suppose you'll have to figure out how think faster."

The War Angels and other members of the Vanguard watched from time to time, offering quiet comments but never interfering. Daryas, to his surprise, began offering pointers, correcting his footwork and balance. Smokey still hadn't quite forgiven him, but his usual biting remarks had softened into something resembling grudging respect.

The work was brutal. The mornings started with combat drills, the afternoons with endurance training—running, climbing, pushing his body until his lungs felt like they would burst. Some nights, he barely made it to his cot before collapsing from exhaustion, his muscles screaming in protest.

One afternoon, after a particularly grueling endurance run, he stumbled, catching himself just before he hit the dirt. Smokey, watching from the sidelines, clicked his tongue. "C'mon, Miner, you're supposed to be impressing us."

Cal shot him a glare, forcing himself upright. "Give me a second."

Smokey grinned. "You don't get seconds out there. You're dead, and I get your boots."

Daryas rolled her eyes but reached down to haul Cal back to his feet. "You're getting better. Just slowly."

Cal wiped the sweat from his brow, chest heaving. "Then I keep going."

Cab smirked. "Good answer." At night, when the others rested, Cal stayed up, forcing himself through lessons on tactics, warfare, supply lines.

And then, as though Cal wasn't being pushed already, Corvin stepped in about a month into his new routine.

It started subtly, like a test. A book left on his cot—basic virology, dry and dense, the kind of thing most soldiers wouldn't give a second glance. But Cal wasn't most soldiers. He read it cover to cover, making notes in the margins. Then another book appeared, this one on immunology, then another on the effects of rapid viral mutations.

One night, Corvin found him in the mess tent, bent over a table covered in notes, scribbling calculations onto a worn scrap of paper. The scientist folded his arms, watching. "You understand more than I expected."

Cal didn't look up. "That supposed to be a compliment?"

"It's an observation." Corvin pulled out a chair and sat across from him. "You don't just read—you absorb. You process. You see patterns where others don't. That's not common."

Cal set his pencil down and rubbed his eyes. "And?"

Corvin smirked. "And that means it's time to take this beyond books."

From that night forward, Cal's routine expanded. Mornings were combat drills, midday was endurance training, and nights were spent in the makeshift research lab, poring over samples and data under Corvin's careful instruction.

The first time he saw an active sample of the virus under a microscope, his stomach twisted. It writhed—alive, aggressive, adapting even as they studied it. Corvin pointed out the patterns in its structure, showing how it mutated in response to stress, how it seemed almost designed to resist containment.

"It learns," Corvin said simply, adjusting the slide. "And so must we."

Cal started assisting in real experiments, mixing compounds under Corvin's guidance, testing resistance factors in controlled environments. He wasn't just memorizing anymore—he was applying. His hands, once made for breaking rock, now measured delicate chemical solutions with precision. His mind, once trained to count ore loads, now mapped viral sequences and reaction chains.

He made mistakes. The first time he miscalculated a dilution, the entire sample batch was rendered useless. Corvin didn't berate him, just handed him another set of vials and made him start over. "Failure is only useless if you don't learn from it. Try again."

There were nights where exhaustion dragged at him, where the weight of training and study became unbearable. His body screamed for rest, his vision blurred over chemical equations and viral strain charts, but he refused to stop. Every moment mattered. Every answer brought him closer to understanding the war in ways no one else seemed to.

And then one night, after hours of poring over old research logs, his mind latched onto something. A mistake.

A simple miscalculation in one of the old formulas. A dilution error—so small that no one had caught it before. He blinked, retracing the math, his pulse picking up. It was wrong. But if it was wrong, then that meant...

He flipped back through the notes, double-checking. The existing formulas assumed the virus's replication rate was linear, but the real-time data they had gathered suggested something else. The virus didn't just spread—it embedded itself into neural pathways faster than anticipated. Which meant if they timed it right—if they administered treatment before the brain fully lost control—

Cal shot to his feet, nearly knocking over the stack of notes. "Corvin!"

Corvin looked up from his own workstation, barely reacting to Cal's outburst. "If you've broken something, don't bother announcing it. Just fix it."

Cal shook his head, gripping the notebook. "No, it's—look at this. The treatment failure rate isn't because the cure doesn't work. It's because we've been administering it too late. The virus doesn't kill its host outright—it rewires them, keeps the body functioning while overriding the brain. If we catch it fast enough—before that transition—"

Corvin's eyes darkened as he scanned the notes, his fingers tapping idly against the table. "That's an interesting theory, but theory doesn't save lives. We need proof."

Cal exhaled, pressing his hands to the table. "Then let's prove it."

Chapter 14 – Proof of Concept

The breakthrough changed everything. Almost.

After weeks of exhaustive research, failures, and near-constant exhaustion, Cal had finally found the missing piece. The virus didn't kill its host before turning them—it rewired them. That meant their approach had been all wrong. The cure wasn't failing; they were simply administering it too late. If they could catch it early enough—before the infection fully hijacked the brain—then there was a chance.

But there were limitations.

The window for treatment was small. Minutes at best. And that was assuming they could administer it at all in the chaos of a battlefield.

The weight of that realization settled in as he sat in the lab, staring at the formula scribbled on the notepad in front of him. Corvin was standing by, his expression unreadable as he reviewed the notes. He hadn't said much since Cal's outburst the night before, but now he slowly nodded.

"It's a step forward," Corvin admitted. "But you understand the problem, don't you?"

Cal exhaled, rubbing his eyes. "Yeah. We're too slow."

"Exactly." Corvin set the notes down and leaned forward. "And now you have to think beyond just solving a problem. You have to think about implementation. How do you get this into soldiers on the field? How do you distribute it in the middle of combat and quickly? Because if you can't answer that, this discovery is worthless."

Cal wanted to argue, but he couldn't. Corvin was right. It wasn't enough to know the answer. It had to be usable.

The next few weeks blurred together. Research turned into testing, which turned into failure after failure. The inoculation had to be refined, the delivery method streamlined. The medical teams ran live trials on infected tissue, searching for the exact moment the cure lost effectiveness. Every failure came with mounting frustration, each setback a reminder that people were still dying while they were stuck in a lab running tests.

The problem wasn't just timing—it was delivery. Needles were too slow. Inhalants weren't reliable. If they were going to make this work, they needed something instantaneous, something that could be deployed the moment an infection took hold. Cal spent long nights sketching out ideas, cross-referencing with old medical data and experimental drug delivery systems. He lost track of how many hours he spent hunched over a desk, reading until his vision blurred.

Then, finally, progress.

"Auto-injectors," Cal muttered one night, staring down at the rough sketches he had drawn. "Pre-loaded doses, pressurized deployment. Soldiers could carry them on their belts, administer them the second they're exposed."

Corvin looked over his shoulder, nodding slowly. "That could work. You think you can refine it?"

"I have to."

Cal threw himself into the new challenge, testing prototypes, refining dosages, adjusting the chemical makeup of the cure to ensure it worked as fast as possible. There were setbacks—some doses degraded too quickly, others weren't potent enough. But with every failure, he learned. With every mistake, he adjusted. His ability to process information, to absorb and apply knowledge, was becoming razor-sharp. He wasn't just thinking like a soldier anymore—he was thinking like a scientist.

Varek noticed.

One evening, after an extended combat session, Cal was just about to head back to the lab when he found himself intercepted. Varek stood near the command tent, arms crossed, watching him with that unreadable expression.

"Walk with me," Varek said.

Cal hesitated but nodded, falling into step beside him. The camp was quieter at this hour; the fires burning low as soldiers took what rest they could. The weight of the past few months hung over all of them.

"You're pushing yourself harder than anyone here," Varek observed. "Most men break under half of what you're doing."

"I don't have the option to break," Cal replied, his voice steadier than he felt. "Not anymore."

Varek hummed. "That's what you think. But even steel has its limits. You're running toward something, Miner. Or maybe you're running from something."

Cal's jaw tightened. "I'm doing what needs to be done."

Varek stopped walking, turning to face him. "Are you? Or are you trying to prove something to ghosts?"

Cal froze, his breath catching in his throat. He wanted to snap back, to argue, but the words wouldn't come. Because Varek wasn't wrong.

The silence stretched between them before Varek finally sighed. "I didn't bring you into this to burn yourself out. If you're serious about this path, you need to learn discipline. Pushing forward blindly will get you killed."

Cal swallowed hard, forcing himself to nod. He knew Varek wasn't saying this to discourage him. If anything, this was the closest thing to concern he had shown.

Varek studied him for a moment longer, then gestured toward the camp. "Go eat. Get some sleep. Tomorrow, we start refining this cure—and we start figuring out how to use it on the battlefield."

The transport rattled over uneven ground, the reinforced plating groaning slightly with every jolt. Inside, the War Angels sat in practiced silence, their armor casting faint reflections against the dim interior lighting. The only sound was the occasional click of a weapon check or the low hum of the transport's engine.

Cal sat between Smokey and Cab, his rifle resting against his knee. He had gone through every step of the mission briefing in his head, memorized the approach, the evac routes, the tactical objectives. But no amount of planning could prepare him for what lay ahead.

Daryas tapped the side of her helmet, activating her comms. Her voice crackled through the earpieces of the team, cutting clean through the hum of the transport's engine. "ETA five minutes. Get your heads on straight. If there are survivors, we get them out. If they're already turning, we test the cure. If it doesn't work, we put them down. No hesitation."

The radio static hissed briefly before stabilizing. "Confirming tactical frequency," Rich's voice came through, casual but focused. "No comm failures this time, yeah?"

"Let's hope not," Smokey muttered. "Last thing we need is another blackout mid-op."

Daryas didn't entertain the side chatter. "Keep channels clear unless necessary. You all know the drill. Eyes up, safeties off."

The transport jolted as it slowed to a crawl, the sound of the engine shifting into a lower gear as they neared the site. The doors groaned as they unlocked, and in an instant, the War

Angels were on their feet, weapons raised, moving with synchronized efficiency.

Cal followed, stepping into the cold, open air.

The outpost was a wreck.

The wind howled through the skeletal remains of buildings, rattling broken shutters and sending loose debris skittering across the ground. The perimeter walls were breached in multiple places, jagged holes exposing the ruins to the open landscape. What little remained of the once-defensible position had been reclaimed by silence. Not the distant moans of the infected. Not the scurry of scavengers or the chatter of survivors. Just silence.

It was the kind of quiet that set nerves on edge.

Daryas raised a fist, and the War Angels froze in place, their weapons sweeping the area. Each Vanguard had their squad fanned out behind them, moving with calculated precision. This wasn't just another clearing operation—this was a recovery, and that meant they had to be careful. Whatever had happened here had left no survivors. Or at least, none that had made themselves known.

"Rich, take your team east. Sweep the outer buildings," Daryas ordered through the comms. "Cab, take the north section and secure a fallback position. Smokey, you and Grassie cover the rear—no blind spots. Cal, with me."

Cal nodded, gripping his rifle as he followed Daryas deeper into the ruins. The further they moved, the heavier the air became. The signs of battle were everywhere—dried blood smeared across walls, bullet casings scattered in thick clusters, broken weapons and discarded gear. But no bodies.

That was the part that unsettled him most.

"They should be here," he muttered, scanning the empty streets.

Daryas' voice crackled in his earpiece. "Stay sharp. If they're not here, that means something moved them."

A beat of silence, then Grassie's voice came through the comms, quieter but carrying an edge of unease. "Or they moved themselves."

The words sent a shiver down Cal's spine. The infected didn't carry their victims away. They didn't feed on the fallen, didn't leave corpses torn apart. Their goal was always the same—to spread, to turn, to convert every last survivor into something mindless, something lost. So where were they?

This wasn't just another outbreak—it was something else.

A metallic clang echoed through the ruins.

Cal's breath hitched, and he swung his rifle toward the sound. The War Angels did the same, their weapons locked on a collapsed structure to their left. The wind picked up again, whistling through gaps in the broken walls.

"Could be debris shifting," Smokey murmured over comms. "Or just this place settling into whatever the hell it's become."

Cal swallowed hard. He had seen infected before—studied their movements from a distance, analyzed their patterns in controlled settings—but this was different. This was the first time he had stepped into a place that felt like it should still be occupied, yet wasn't. The absence of life, the unnatural silence, the emptiness—it felt wrong. Like the moment before a storm hit, when the air was too still, the pressure too heavy. The kind of fear that gnawed at the gut and refused to let go.

Daryas motioned for him to move forward. "You're here to observe, right? Time to start observing."

Cal tightened his grip on his weapon and stepped forward, inching toward the collapsed building. The others followed, covering him from a distance. Each step sent dust swirling around his boots, the crunch of debris underfoot too loud in the suffocating quiet.

Then something shifted in the shadows.

A figure—just barely visible through a narrow gap in the rubble.

It didn't move like the infected. It didn't lunge, didn't growl. It just... watched.

Cal raised a fist, signaling a halt. His pulse thundered in his ears.

"I think we've got a survivor."

The survivor wasn't infected—just injured.

Cal let out a breath he hadn't realized he was holding as he knelt beside the soldier, taking in their pale complexion, the sweat clinging to their forehead. A makeshift bandage wrapped around their thigh, but it was soaked through with dried blood. They had been here for a while. Alone. Waiting.

"You're lucky we found you," Cal murmured as he reached for his medical pack. "Stay still. We'll get you patched up."

The soldier's lips parted, their voice barely a whisper. "Thought... thought I was the last one."

Cal's stomach twisted at the words. "You're not. We're still looking."

Daryas knelt beside them, pressing a hand to her earpiece. "Rich, get a team on this one. He's stable, but he won't be moving on his own. Get him back to the transport for treatment."

"Copy that," came the reply. Within moments, two soldiers jogged in, securing the wounded man onto a stretcher before disappearing into the ruins with him. Cal watched them go before turning back to Daryas.

"We keep moving."

Pushing deeper into the stronghold, the team pressed on. The silence was pressing, thick with the weight of the unknown. The further they moved, the more it felt like the ruins were holding their breath.

Then, over comms: "We've got something."

Smokey's voice was sharp, focused. "Locked door on the west side of the admin building. Heat signatures inside. Could be survivors."

Daryas didn't hesitate. "We're on our way. Hold position."

Cal's heart pounded as they navigated the debris, the ruins pressing in around them like a tomb. The distant creak of shifting metal echoed through the hollow structures, the sound sharp against the suffocating silence. Somewhere, wind whistled through a shattered window frame, making a low, haunting wail. It felt like the stronghold itself was breathing—waiting.

Each step kicked up layers of dust, disturbing the untouched remnants of a battle long since over. Bullet holes riddled the walls, long-dried blood smeared in erratic streaks. A tattered banner bearing the coalition insignia hung limp from a half-collapsed beam, swaying slightly in the stale air. Cal forced himself to focus, keeping his grip firm on his rifle as they approached the admin building.

When they reached the door, Smokey was already there, his rifle steady, Grassie covering him. The building loomed over them, its windows black voids staring out like empty eyes.

"Movement inside," Smokey said, nodding toward the heat scanner strapped to his wrist. "It's not erratic, so they're probably not infected. But they're not exactly making themselves known, either."

Cal swallowed hard, his throat dry. The idea of survivors huddled inside this husk of a stronghold sent a chill through him. What kind of hell had they been living in?

He pressed his hand against the rusted metal, feeling the cold bite of it beneath his fingertips. Two slow knocks. "Coalition forces. If you're alive, you need to let us know."

Silence.

Then—

A faint scraping sound. Like something dragging along the floor.

Distant shuffling. A sharp inhale.

Then finally, a voice, weak and barely more than a whisper: "Help us."

Smokey glanced at Daryas, his jaw set. She gave a nod. "Breach it."

Smokey didn't hesitate. He stepped back, raised his rifle, and fired a precise shot into the locking mechanism. The shot rang out like thunder in the dead air. The door groaned as it gave way, swinging inward with a long, tortured creak.

The smell hit them first.

Stale sweat. Fear. Blood. The kind of scent that settled into a place and never left. It was thick, cloying, sinking into their skin.

Inside, a small group of survivors huddled in the corner, shielding their eyes from the sudden exposure. Their faces were gaunt, their clothes filthy, their hands trembling. Some looked relieved. Others looked too far gone to register what was happening. Their eyes darted between the soldiers, untrusting, hollowed out by weeks—maybe months—of living in fear.

Cal stepped in cautiously, his voice steady but low. "You're safe now. We're getting you out of here."

One of the survivors—a woman with hollowed-out eyes—staggered forward, her steps unsteady. "It's over?"

"We're getting you to safety," Daryas confirmed. "But we need to move now."

The survivors didn't argue. They followed orders, moving in a tight formation as the War Angels guided them back toward the transports. The mission was almost done.

Then Cal felt it before he saw it.

A shift in the air. A wrongness that prickled at the back of his neck.

A dull, wet thud.

The air filled with pink mist.

Cal barely had time to react before his world tilted. The first thing he registered was the burning in his throat—sharp, acrid, as if he had inhaled something rotten. Then came the sound—a horrible gasping wail, rising up from the mist like a chorus of the dying.

Gunfire erupted around him. The Angels were moving, their weapons lighting up the fogged air as figures emerged from the edges of the ruins. Shadows lurched from the smoke, moving with unnatural speed, their limbs contorting in sudden, jerking motions. The first infected dropped as a shot tore through its skull, but more kept coming. A horde.

"We're compromised!" Smokey shouted over the gunfire. "Move, move!"

Cal tried to move, but his body wasn't responding fast enough. The mist was sinking into him, crawling through his lungs. His limbs felt heavy, his vision blurred at the edges. He could hear the others shouting, feel the vibrations of their gunfire through the cracked pavement beneath him.

Then he saw the figures coming toward him.

Not shambling. Not slow. Fast. Too fast.

He stumbled, his legs nearly giving out, but he caught himself at the last second. His breath came in short, ragged gasps. No, not like this.

His hand shot to his belt, fingers fumbling for the injector. He could feel the mist burrowing into him, the sickness curling in his veins. His vision swam. He wasn't going to make it.

His hand found the injector.

He jammed it into his arm and pressed the release.

A sharp sting. A rush of cold through his veins. A moment of clarity.

Then—

Nothing.

Darkness swallowed him whole.

Chapter 15 – A Whisper In the Dark

The world came back in fragments—sound before sight, pressure before pain.

The world was distant, muffled. A dull beeping echoed somewhere nearby, rhythmic and steady. Cal's breath hitched as he gasped awake, the sharp sting of antiseptic flooding his senses. The air was cold, sterile, and his skin itched from where wires had been attached to his arm. He tried to move, but his limbs felt sluggish, weighted like they didn't belong to him.

He wasn't alone.

A figure stood at the foot of his cot, scribbling something onto a data pad. The white coat was a giveaway—it wasn't Corvin. It was a doctor. One of the medical personnel assigned to critical cases.

"He's awake," the doctor muttered, not even looking at Cal. A second later, the man pressed a button on his wrist communicator. "Corvin, your subject is conscious."

Cal's stomach twisted at the phrasing. *Subject.* Like he was some lab experiment. Before he could process that thought further, the tent flap rustled.

Corvin entered like he had been waiting for this moment, hands clasped behind his back, eyes sharp with intrigue. He spared the doctor only a glance before stepping toward Cal's cot. He was lying on a cot, the hum of machinery nearby. His vision swam, the overhead lights glaring against the dull ache in his skull. His limbs felt heavy, sluggish, but nothing was wrong. No pain, no burning fever. Just exhaustion.

He was alive.

More than that—the cure had worked.

A shadow moved beside him. Cal turned his head and found Corvin standing there, arms crossed, watching him like an experiment that had just yielded an interesting result.

"You look intact," Corvin said dryly. "That's promising."

Cal swallowed, his throat raw. "I—" His voice cracked, and he had to try again. "I was exposed."

"Yes," Corvin confirmed. "Directly. You were drowning in it. Yet here you are."

Cal exhaled, staring up at the ceiling. It worked. The cure actually worked. If it had been even a second slower…

Corvin took a step closer, eyes narrowing slightly. "How soon did you inject yourself?"

"Seconds."

A slow nod. "Then we know the window holds. No lingering symptoms?"

Cal shook his head, still groggy. "I don't know yet." His limbs felt heavy, his thoughts sluggish. His body wasn't screaming in pain, but something felt off, like he was still catching up to what had happened. He flexed his fingers, then pressed a hand to his forehead. "Just… tired, I think."

Corvin finally exhaled, rubbing his chin. "Good. That means we have confirmation—the treatment is viable if used immediately. And you, Miner, just became more valuable than you were yesterday."

Cal clenched his jaw at that. "Glad I could be of use."

Corvin smirked. "Oh, don't pretend this wasn't useful to you, too. Now you know. Now we all know." He gestured toward the medical monitors, still tracking Cal's vitals. "You're the proof the cure works. No fever, no symptoms, no lingering effects. We expected this, of course—but having live verification always helps."

Cal sat up, his mind racing. He'd survived, but what about the others? The War Angels? The survivors?

He swung his legs off the cot, trying to stand. Corvin didn't stop him, just watched as Cal steadied himself. "They're fine," Corvin said, as if reading his thoughts. "The Angels secured the survivors and held off the infected long enough to get back. The stronghold, however, is lost."

Cal clenched his fists. Another stronghold fallen. Another place erased.

He hesitated before speaking, keeping his tone casual. "Funny thing, isn't it? Strongholds move, and it's like they were never there. You'd think we'd leave something behind."

Corvin's expression didn't change. "Elaborate."

Cal shrugged, watching Corvin carefully. "I mean, when we left our last position, we scrubbed it clean. Tracks covered, fires put out, every sign of human life erased. And now this place? Completely overrun, wiped away. It's like none of them ever existed."

A long pause. Corvin's eyes were unreadable, but something flickered there. A calculation.

"That's standard procedure," Corvin said smoothly. "Leaving a stronghold intact after a fall is an invitation for more casualties. We ensure nothing remains that can be used against us—by the infected or otherwise."

Cal tilted his head, feigning casual curiosity. "Too bad we can't just purge the stronghold off the map. Make sure nothing gets left behind."

There it was. The word. *Purge.*

Corvin's fingers twitched—small, barely noticeable, but Cal caught it. His expression remained neutral, but for the first time, there was a hesitation before he answered. Not long, just enough for Cal to know he had registered the word.

Corvin's gaze met his, measuring. "That's not how we operate."

Cal shrugged. "Shame. It'd be cleaner that way."

Another pause. Then Corvin let out a low exhale, his posture relaxing, as if dismissing the idea. "The objective isn't to erase history, Miner. It's to move forward without unnecessary burdens."

Cal didn't respond. *Because now, he knew.*

Cal nodded slowly, pretending to accept the answer. But now, he was sure of it. Corvin knew more than he let on.

Before he could say anything else, the tent flap rustled, and Varek stepped in. His gaze flicked to Corvin before settling on Cal.

"Good," Varek said. "You're up. Get dressed. We're debriefing in five."

Cal exhaled and nodded, grabbing his gear. There wasn't time to process everything. There never was.

The debrief was short and direct. The mission had been a partial success—*they recovered survivors, but the stronghold itself was overrun beyond saving.* The virus bombs were getting worse, the infected more coordinated. And now, there was proof the cure worked, but only if deployed immediately.

Cal sat in the command tent, listening to the rundown as Varek addressed the War Angels. Smokey leaned against a crate nearby, arms crossed, while Grassie was already busy picking at a food ration like she hadn't just come back from a warzone. Rich, as always, stood silent, helmet on.

Cal shifted, trying to push down the lingering unease in his gut. Something about the attack didn't sit right. *The infected had been waiting. They weren't just reacting; they had been positioned.*

Varek spoke again, pulling him from his thoughts. "The cure changes things. Now that we know it works, we have to figure out distribution."

Corvin nodded. "We'll need a mobile deployment system. Something that can be carried by squads and used in real-time."

Varek folded his arms. "That's the next step, then. Corvin, I want field tests started immediately. We don't deploy this cure wide-scale until we know it won't compromise a soldier mid-fight."

Corvin gave a slight smirk. "Wouldn't want that."

Varek ignored him and turned back to the Angels. "We adapt. This won't change the war overnight. But if we integrate it properly, it can keep our soldiers in the fight longer."

Smokey exhaled, shaking his head. "So we get to live just long enough to die another day. Great."

Grassie nudged him, chewing on her ration. "Better than turning."

Varek ignored their exchange. "You're dismissed. Get some rest. Cal, stay behind."

The War Angels stood and filed out. Smokey gave Cal a sidelong glance before leaving, followed by Grassie and Cab. Rich was the last to go, his imposing frame pausing briefly before stepping outside.

Varek waited until they were gone before speaking. "That was your first combat mission, Miner. How do you feel?"

Cal straightened. "Like I need to be better."

Varek studied him for a moment, then gave a slight nod. "Good. Get some rest. I expect you back at training tomorrow."

Cal gave a short nod, then turned on his heel and left the command tent, stepping into the cold night air. The fires around the encampment had burned low, leaving long shadows stretching across the makeshift roads between tents and supply crates. Soldiers milled about, some heading to the mess, others standing watch. It was the usual routine after a mission—patch wounds, reload weapons, pretend like they weren't all waiting for the next fight.

He adjusted the strap on his gear, ready to head toward the barracks, when he spotted a soldier lingering just beyond the edge of the main encampment. The man wasn't standing at attention, wasn't talking to anyone—just waiting.

Cal slowed as he approached, instincts flaring. The soldier glanced up, eyes sharp but cautious. "Walk with me."

Cal hesitated. He didn't recognize the man—at least, not immediately. But there was no alarm in his posture, no attempt to appear anything but calm.

"Who are you?"

"Not important," the soldier muttered. "What I have for you is."

Cal's jaw tightened, but he followed as the soldier led him down a narrow path between supply containers, away from the ears of patrols. When they were alone, the man reached into his pocket and pulled out a small, black data chip. He held it out.

"One of the survivors told me to give this to you. Said it was important."

Cal stared at it. *Why me?* Not Varek. Not Corvin. Him.

Slowly, he took the chip, turning it over in his fingers. The markings on the side were unmistakably Coalition-issued, but old. Worn. Whatever was on this wasn't new intel.

The soldier took a step back. "I don't know what's on it. Just know they were desperate for you to have it. Be careful."

Then he turned and disappeared into the night.

Cal looked down at the chip in his hand. His stomach twisted with something he couldn't name—anticipation, dread. This wasn't just another battle report.

This was a piece of the bigger picture.

And for the first time, he wasn't sure he wanted to know what came next.

Chapter 16 – The Breaking Point

Cal sat on the edge of his cot, turning the data chip over in his fingers. The weight of it felt heavier than it should, as if it carried the burden of whatever information was locked inside. He should have gone straight to sleep—Varek had ordered him back to training the next morning—but there was no shutting off his mind now.

His tent was dimly lit, a single lamp casting long shadows against the canvas walls. The low murmur of soldiers outside was distant, almost comforting in its routine. For them, life moved forward. For him, it felt like something had shifted, like he was standing on the edge of something he wasn't sure he wanted to step into.

He had two choices: take this to Varek and Corvin and let them decide what came next—or open it himself.

The decision wasn't really a choice at all.

With a slow exhale, Cal reached for the portable terminal beside his cot and slid the data chip into the reader. The screen flickered to life, lines of encrypted code filling the display. His fingers hovered over the controls. If this was meant for him, then why?

The decryption process was slow. The software wasn't standard Coalition tech—it was older, patched together, and designed to be accessed manually. Whoever had given him this chip had wanted it hidden.

Then, the first files unlocked—but only in fragments.

Cal's breath hitched as he scanned the information. Deployment orders. Timelines. Communications between commanding officers—some of them weeks old. But it wasn't just standard reports. There were messages that shouldn't exist, references to strongholds before they fell, movements of infected before the attacks happened.

But the information was incomplete. Some of the messages were cut off mid-sentence, the encryption blocking entire sections of data. It was as if he had walked into a room full of maps with half the markings erased. Whatever was on here, it was important enough to be hidden, even from whoever had managed to extract this much.

At the bottom of the list, two words sent a chill through his veins: Phase Two Initiated.

But no explanation. No context.

Cal's hands tightened into fists. He scrolled further, his pulse hammering in his ears. Although fragmented, the messages' implication was clear. The attacks weren't random. The infected weren't just stumbling upon strongholds by chance.

Something or, the-more horrifying idea - *Someone* was guiding them.

A sharp knock at the entrance to his quarters made him flinch.

Cal reached for his sidearm, tensing, but when the tent flap pushed open, Daryas stepped in. Her helmet was off, dark strands of hair falling loose from where she'd tied it back. Her eyes immediately flicked to the terminal, narrowing.

"That doesn't look like sleep," she muttered.

Cal exhaled sharply. "Wasn't tired."

She didn't buy it, stepping closer. "What is that?"

For a moment, Cal debated closing the file. But then he turned the screen so she could see. Daryas scanned the messages, her expression tightening. Her eyes flicked over the fragmented reports, her brow furrowing deeper with each missing line. When she looked back at him, there was no sarcasm, no casual remark.

"Where did you get this?"

"One of the survivors. Said it was important."

She let out a quiet curse, then crossed her arms. "Does Varek know?"

Cal hesitated. "No."

Daryas exhaled through her nose, glancing toward the tent flap as if making sure no one was listening. Her fingers hovered over the edge of the terminal screen. "But this doesn't make sense, Cal. If this is real, why didn't the survivor give it to Varek? Why you?"

Cal hesitated before answering. "I think whoever gave this to me knew something we don't. And for reasons I think we can guess they didn't trust command with it."

Daryas exhaled sharply, rubbing a hand down her face. "If this is encrypted, we need a command-level decryption key to open it fully. Varek has one. If we ask him for it—"

Cal shook his head. "He'll want to know why. And if Corvin gets involved, we'll never see this data again."

Daryas' jaw tightened, but she didn't respond immediately. Cal could see the gears turning in her head, the instinct to follow orders warring with the uncomfortable reality sitting in front of her.

He inhaled sharply and leaned forward. "Listen, just look at the pattern for a second."

Daryas gave him a hard look but didn't interrupt.

Cal gestured to the screen, his breath coming faster now, the pieces snapping together all at once. "Every time we abandon a stronghold, we wipe it clean. We erase everything—like we were never there. We do that to our own bases, but these other places? They're just... gone. Like they were meant to fall."

Daryas frowned, but Cal wasn't done. "Back at the last stronghold, where we killed the Grave Titan, we overheard survivors talking about something called a 'purge.' At the time, I didn't understand what they meant, but then I started putting the pieces together. We scrub our own strongholds before we move, but what if something else is wiping out the others after we leave? And when I asked Varek about it, he shut me down so fast it was like I'd stepped on a landmine."

Daryas' expression didn't change, but her eyes flicked back to the screen. She was listening now.

"Then there's Corvin," Cal pressed. "The way he reacted when I tested him with that word—'purge'—he hesitated. Corvin doesn't hesitate, Daryas. He calculates. He adapts. But for a split second, he didn't know what to say. That's not nothing."

Daryas exhaled, rubbing a hand down her face, but Cal kept going. He needed her to understand. "And what about the virus itself? I told Corvin it looked engineered. And what did he do? He shut me down. Not denied it. Just... ended the conversation. Steered me away. Every time I get close to seeing the bigger picture, someone pulls me back."

Daryas crossed her arms, her stance shifting. "And now you think this Phase Two is part of it?"

"I don't know what it is," Cal admitted. "But I know it's not random. And someone didn't want us to find out about it. They trusted me with this chip. Not Varek. Not Corvin. Me. That means something."

Daryas was quiet for a long time, her jaw tight. She was trained to follow orders. To trust the system. But she wasn't stupid. And Cal could see the war inside her—the part of her that wanted to dismiss all of this warring with the part that saw what he saw.

Then, finally, she muttered, "That leaves us one option."

Cal nodded. "We find a fallen command center. Get a key from there."

She let out a quiet curse. "You realize how dangerous that is."

"Do we have a choice?"

She stared at the screen for another long moment before finally sighing. "We'll need a plan. And we need to make sure no one questions why we're leaving. We need a mission."

Cal swallowed, the weight of her words settling in. Because if what they had just found was true, then everything they thought they knew about the war was a lie. And now, they were going to have to prove it themselves.

Cal stepped out of the tent, inhaling the cool night air, trying to clear his head. The camp was quieter now, the fires burning low, casting flickering shadows along the pathways between tents and supply crates. Soldiers moved in the dim light, some on patrol, others tending to weapons or simply sitting in exhausted silence.

He needed to walk. To think. To process.

Before he could take more than a few steps, a familiar voice called out.

"Hey!"

Cal turned to see Joran jogging up to him, hands stuffed into his jacket pockets, his face split between a grin and something uncertain. "Figured I'd find you wandering off on your own."

Cal let out a short breath, trying to muster a smirk but failing. "Just needed air."

Joran fell into step beside him. "Yeah, well, if you were looking to sneak off, you're terrible at it. Thought you could use some company."

Cal didn't respond right away. He just walked, listening to the distant hum of the camp, letting the silence stretch. Joran didn't seem to mind at first, but after a few minutes, he sighed.

"So, what's going on with you, man?" Joran asked, kicking a loose rock along the path. "You're always busy, always with the War Angels or Varek or whoever. You don't even come by anymore. Feels like I lost my best friend, and he's still standing right here."

Cal clenched his jaw. He had known this conversation was coming, but it still hit harder than he expected. "I've been training. There's a lot going on."

Joran let out a dry laugh. "Yeah, no kidding. You're a soldier now. And not just a soldier, but one of them. The kind of people we used to joke about when we were working the mines. The kind of people who barely looked at us."

Cal's stomach twisted, but he kept his face neutral. "It's different now."

Joran shook his head. "Yeah, it is. But I don't even know who you are anymore. We used to talk about everything. Now? I barely see you, and when I do, it's like you're always somewhere else."

Cal exhaled, rubbing his temples. He wanted to tell Joran everything. About the chip. About the truth he was starting to unravel. About how he was terrified that whatever they found next would change everything again. But he couldn't. If what he feared was true, this wasn't just dangerous—it was suicidal.

"Joran... there are things I can't talk about right now. Not because I don't want to, but because if I do—" He stopped himself, shaking his head. "It's bigger than us."

Joran stared at him, his jaw tightening. "Bigger than us? Since when did that mean shutting me out? You think I don't get it? That I don't see what's happening? You act like you're the only one who's ever lost something, but I lost people, too. We all did. You're not special, Cal. You just stopped caring about the rest of us."

Cal flinched like he'd been struck. "That's not true."

"Isn't it?" Joran shot back. "You don't even try anymore. You have new friends. New orders. You've got something that matters to you now, and it sure as hell isn't the people you grew up with."

Cal clenched his fists, biting down the instinct to lash out. Joran was hurt. And he had every right to be.

"I'm trying to keep people alive," Cal said, voice quieter now. "That's all I can say. And if I tell you more, I put you in danger."

Joran scoffed, stepping back. "Right. Because now you get to decide what's too dangerous for me?" He shook his head, his voice thick with something between frustration and sorrow. "Guess I really don't know you anymore."

Cal looked away. He wanted to fix this, but he couldn't. Not yet.

Joran exhaled, shoving his hands deeper into his pockets. "Whatever, man. Hope whatever you're chasing is worth it."

Then he turned and walked away.

Cal watched him go, a hollow feeling settling deep in his chest. The war had taken a lot from him.

Now, it had taken Joran, too.

Chapter 17 – A Door Left Open

The days that followed felt almost normal—almost.

Cal returned to his training schedule, throwing himself back into the routine of drills, weapons exercises, and combat simulations. Every morning, he woke up before dawn, ran with the squads, sparred with the War Angels, and by midday, he was back in the lab, poring over research and refining their delivery systems for the cure. On the surface, he was just another soldier again.

But every move he made was calculated.

He and Daryas couldn't afford to rush. If they were going to break away and search for the decryption key at a fallen command center, they needed a reason to leave. One that wouldn't raise suspicion.

It started with small conversations, planting ideas. Maybe another stronghold had abandoned supplies they could salvage. Maybe old command centers had tech that could help with the cure. The ideas weren't fabricated—there was truth to them—but they had to be introduced carefully. A mission like this needed to be Varek's idea, not theirs.

Daryas played her part well. She was measured, careful, never pressing too hard. When she spoke with Varek, it was casual—a passing comment about scouting new locations, securing old medical caches. She never outright suggested a mission. She let the idea take root, let it become something command might think was their own. Meanwhile, Cal focused on the lab, working harder than ever to appear occupied, appear committed.

But he never stopped watching.

Corvin, as always, was methodical in his work. He barely seemed to register anything beyond research and results. But Varek? Varek was watching Cal. Not suspiciously, not overtly, but with that same assessing look he always had, as if he was waiting for something.

Cal didn't let it shake him. He just kept moving forward.

One evening, after another long day, he found himself back at the shooting range, running drills alone. The repetitive motion was grounding, something he could control. Load, aim, fire. Adjust stance. Again. The targets weren't the problem. The thoughts in his head were.

The crunch of boots on gravel made him glance to the side. Daryas stood a few feet away, arms crossed.

"You're overthinking," she said.

Cal sighed, lowering his rifle. "I don't have much of a choice."

Daryas stepped up beside him, watching as he reloaded. "We'll get our shot. We just have to be patient."

Cal exhaled through his nose. "Patience isn't my strong suit."

Daryas smirked slightly. "Yeah. I noticed."

She picked up a discarded rifle from the rack and tested the weight, glancing at him. "You've gotten better. Your stance is tighter. Less wasted motion."

"That's the idea," Cal muttered, reloading.

A pause settled between them, the distant sounds of the camp filling the quiet. Soldiers laughing, murmuring. Life moving forward, like it always did. Like it was supposed to.

Daryas finally broke the silence. "You eat today?"

Cal shot her a look. "What kind of question is that?"

She shrugged, unbothered. "A relevant one. You look like you haven't slept in a week, and the last time I saw you sit down to eat something that wasn't a nutrient bar was... when?"

Cal sighed. "I'm fine."

"That's not an answer."

He hesitated, then smirked slightly. "Alright, mom. I'll get some food."

Cal felt a pang of loss. He hadn't thought of his mother in months, but he let it pass. There were bigger problems in front of him she would want him focused on.

Daryas rolled her eyes but gave a small nod. "Good. I don't need you passing out mid-mission."

She set the rifle back down and turned to leave, then paused. "We'll get our shot at this. You know that, right?"

Cal exhaled. "Yeah. I know."

"Then stop overthinking and trust that we will."

Cal left the shooting range, his body aching from the repetitive strain of drills, but his mind was the real problem. Even as the night air cooled his skin, his thoughts kept cycling through every word Daryas had said. They had to be patient. Had to be smart. Had to play their roles until the time was right. But the waiting was suffocating.

Cal found himself wandering toward the mess hall, his stomach reminding him that, despite everything Daryas was right, he still needed to eat. The structure itself was nothing more than a repurposed prefab warehouse, lined with long metal tables and crates stacked high with ration supplies. Dim lighting buzzed overhead, flickering now and then from the inconsistent power grid. The scent of overheated protein packs and stale bread filled the air, a constant reminder that food here was about survival, not comfort.

The place was half-full, soldiers and workers eating in silence, talking in hushed voices, or playing quiet rounds of card games on worn-down tabletops. The war had trained them to keep their heads down—to conserve energy, to avoid unnecessary confrontation. Nobody was laughing, and nobody was wasting food. Everything was functional. Efficient.

Cal grabbed a tray, scanning the room before settling at an empty table in the far corner. He forced himself to eat, chewing mechanically, more out of necessity than hunger. His mind was elsewhere, turning over the mission, the encrypted data, Corvin's watchful gaze.

The scrape of a chair pulled him back to the present.

A man sat across from him—one of the mechanics who worked on the convoy's transports. His uniform was stained with grease, his hands rough with callouses. He wasn't a soldier. He was one of the many who kept the war machine moving but never got a say in where it was going.

"You're starting to look like them, you know," the mechanic said, tearing into a stale protein bar. His voice was calm, casual, but there was something knowing in it.

Cal frowned slightly. "Like who?"

The mechanic nodded toward a nearby table where a group of Vanguard soldiers sat, speaking in low voices. "Them. The officers. The ones who aren't just passing through. You got that same look in your eyes. Like you're watching everything, but not really here."

Cal swallowed his bite of food, setting his utensil down. "I've been busy."

The mechanic let out a quiet chuckle. "Yeah. No doubt." He leaned back slightly, studying Cal. "You used to sit with the rest of us. Back when you were just another worker, another grunt. Now you're always off with the War Angels, always with the big names. Don't think people haven't noticed."

Cal exhaled through his nose. "What's your point?"

The mechanic shrugged. "No point. Just making an observation. People notice things. Thought you should know."

Cal studied him for a moment. He wasn't wrong. He wasn't the same person who had worked beside people like this, sweating in the mines, sharing jokes in between shifts. He had changed.

But could he afford to care about that now?

The mechanic let out a dry chuckle. "See? There it is. That look. You don't know whether to care or ignore it. That's how it starts."

Cal sighed, shoving another bite into his mouth just to end the conversation.

The mechanic stood, tossing his empty tray onto the collection stack. "Well, good talk, Vanguard-in-training. Try not to forget where you came from."

Cal didn't answer.

He sat in the mess for a while longer, picking at his food, feeling the weight of everything pressing down on him.

By the time he stood to leave, he realized he wasn't sure what he hated more—the fact that people were noticing...

Or the fact that he didn't have an answer for them.

The next morning, Cal was halfway through a ration pack when a research assistant stopped at his table. "Corvin wants to see you. Now."

Cal wiped his mouth, forcing himself to move with purpose. He couldn't show hesitation.

The lab was colder than usual, the overhead lights casting a stark glow over the equipment. Corvin stood near a holographic projection of a battlefield map, arms folded behind his back.

Scientists whispered among themselves, reviewing reports, but the room felt heavier than it should have.

Corvin turned when he entered. "Perfect timing." He gestured toward the map. "We've been reviewing supply chains. Some of the sites we lost—particularly abandoned command posts—might still have intact data cores. You see why that matters, don't you?"

Cal kept his posture relaxed, even though his heart pounded. "You think there's something worth recovering?"

Corvin's eyes flickered toward him. "You tell me."

It was a test. A deliberate one. Corvin was always watching for something. Whether it was curiosity, loyalty, or a slip-up, Cal couldn't tell.

Cal glanced at the map. It showed a fallen stronghold about a week's travel away, still marked with restricted access tags. None of the Coalitions they had communications with had sent teams to recover anything yet—too much of a risk, too few resources to spare.

But that meant it was exactly what he and Daryas needed.

Cal kept his tone casual. "If there's intact data, we should retrieve it before the infected tear through whatever's left. Could be valuable for logistics."

Corvin gave a small, unreadable smile. "That's what I was thinking."

He gestured to the map. "Varek is considering a scouting run. He's hesitant—too many unknowns, not enough intel. But if someone were to make a case for it, say… someone who understands the importance of what's inside?"

Cal felt his stomach twist. This was too easy.

Corvin wanted him to push for this mission.

Cal forced a nod. "I'll see what I can do."

Corvin clapped a hand on his shoulder, just once, before stepping away. "Good. And Cal? Be careful what you ask for. Sometimes, the answers aren't what you expect."

The lab door hissed shut behind him, leaving Cal alone with the flickering map.

His stomach twisted. Had Corvin just handed them exactly what they needed? Or was he leading them into something?

Too many variables. Too many unknowns. Whether Corvin was an ally or an enemy, one thing was certain:

They had their excuse to leave.

Now, they just had to make it happen.

Chapter 18 – Into the Storm

The meeting was tense, the kind where the air itself felt thick with something unspoken. Commander Varek stood at the head of the war table, arms crossed, his gaze sweeping over the assembled officers. The holo-map flickered in front of him, displaying the ruins of the fallen stronghold they were discussing. It should have been an easy call—an abandoned site, the potential for usable tech, and a trained team willing to go in.

But Varek wasn't convinced.

Daryas and Cal stood at attention, waiting. The War Angels rarely had to request missions—orders were given, and they executed them. But this was different. This had to be presented just right. Too eager, and Varek would see through it. Too reluctant, and they'd never get sent.

"The site has been dark for months," Varek said at last. His tone was neutral, but there was something else behind it. A hesitation. A reluctance. "There's no guarantee anything is left worth salvaging."

Cal forced himself to keep his expression neutral. "All intelligence says nothing has gone in or out since the day it fell. We won't know unless we go."

Varek's gaze flicked to him, unreadable. "And you think this is a priority?"

Daryas spoke up. "Sir, some of the tech in these command centers is built to survive collapses. If there's anything left intact, it could be useful—not just for research, but for ongoing operations."

"And if there's nothing?" Varek countered. "If you go in and find rubble, wasted effort, and more bodies?"

Cal hesitated. This was where he had to be careful. Varek was testing him.

"Then we confirm it's a loss and move on," he said evenly. "But if there's even a chance of usable tech, isn't it worth taking?"

Varek studied him for a long moment. Then, slowly, he nodded to himself, like he was piecing something together.

Then the tent flap opened, and Corvin stepped inside.

The temperature in the room seemed to drop a degree.

"I hope I'm not interrupting," Corvin said smoothly, though he didn't sound like he cared either way. He moved with the ease of a man who was always where he needed to be, wearing his usual detached expression, his eyes scanning the holo-map before landing on Varek.

"I heard about the stronghold recon mission," Corvin continued. "Seems like an excellent opportunity. The amount of lost technology alone—"

"It's a risk," Varek interrupted. "And it's not one I take lightly."

Corvin smiled, thin and knowing. "No, of course not. But given what we've already invested in the cure, you have to consider the potential benefits. If we recovered additional research logs, data cores—things that could push us forward even further—it would be worth the attempt. Wouldn't you agree?"

Varek's jaw tightened slightly. Cal saw it. The push. The moment of doubt creeping in. Corvin wasn't even trying to be subtle—he was applying pressure, forcing Varek to agree.

And Varek knew it.

But in the end, Varek still nodded.

"Fine. The War Angels go in. No backup, no secondary teams. You get in, confirm what's there, take whatever you can, and get out. Bandit and his team can drop you in, but they won't be waiting around. You'll have to find a way to reach out when you're ready or make the week-long trek back yourself."

Daryas saluted. "Understood, sir."

Cal did the same, keeping his face impassive. On the surface, it was a victory. They had their mission.

But beneath that, it was something else.

Varek hadn't wanted to say yes. And Corvin had made sure he did.

The flyer hummed with tension, but unlike before a mission, it wasn't the silence of focus—it was the kind of quiet that came before a storm. The War Angels sat strapped into their seats, running last-minute gear checks. Across from them, Bandit's squad was far more relaxed.

Jmeli stretched her legs out, arms folded behind her head. "You guys always this broody before a drop? Or is this a special occasion?"

Daryas glanced up. "We like to focus."

"You like to sulk," she corrected with a grin. "Gotta learn to enjoy the ride."

"Hard to enjoy when we don't know what's waiting for us down there," Cab muttered, adjusting the strap on her med kit.

"That's why you have us," Bandit called from the cockpit. "We get you in safe and sound. What happens after that? Not our problem."

Nac leaned forward, tapping his knuckles against the metal frame of the flyer. "You know, it's funny. People always assume

Flyers got it easy. That all we do is drop people off and fly away."

"Not the case?" Cal asked.

"Not a chance," Nac said with a smirk. "First time I ever went out, we dropped a team into what was supposed to be a routine salvage. Whole thing went sideways in the first twenty minutes. We had to pick them up while a Grave Titan was tearing apart the LZ. I was on the turret, unloading everything we had, and you know what that thing did? Just kept going. Like it didn't even register we were trying to stop it. Didn't run, didn't even slow down—just adapted to everything we threw at it."

He leaned back, shaking his head. "That's when I realized—we don't fight to win. We fight to keep the inevitable at bay. Long enough to get people out, long enough to make the next move. Doesn't mean you always walk away. That and ground troops have a hard time fighting against us flyers. Our jet packs make us damn hard to hit. Unless they're running launchers, but that's rare for infected. Other coalitions are the problem there."

"Those are the real fight stories," Jmeli said nodding, but her tone was distracted. She was reliving some kind of vision in the privacy of her mind.

Cal absorbed that. It was rare for a Vanguard to talk about a mission like that. Most just said "you get used to it" and left it at that.

Cal hesitated before speaking, mulling over what Nac had said. He could hear the low hum of the flyer's engines, the occasional clank of a loose strap shifting as the others adjusted their gear. Finally, he glanced at Nac. "So that's where you get your name?"

Nac's smirk widened as he tilted his head slightly. "Not a chance." He let the words settle before continuing, "Someone said it once after a training run—'not a chance that guy misses'—and, well, here we are."

"Could be worse," Jmeli added. "You could've ended up with something like 'Lucky' or 'Deadeye.'"

"Or 'Boots,'" Sib muttered, shaking his head. "Remember that guy?"

Jmeli snickered. "Boots. Poor bastard lost one during a drop and never heard the end of it."

Cal chuckled despite himself, then nodded toward Fafa. "And what about him?"

Jmeli grinned. "Fafa doesn't need a callsign. His reputation speaks for itself."

"That true?" Cal asked.

Fafa didn't respond, just gave a slow, deliberate nod, his expression unreadable.

"See?" Jmeli said. "Man of few words. But when he does talk, you listen."

Cal sat back, letting the conversation settle around him. The easy banter, the way they carried their history in their words—it made the wait feel a little less suffocating. For now, at least, they could pretend they weren't about to jump into a dead stronghold with no guarantee they were coming back out.

Jmeli glanced at Cal, noticing how he kept adjusting the straps on his harness, his fingers twitching slightly. "You ever done a live drop before, Rookie?"

Cal exhaled. "Training runs, but never at full speed."

Sib, who had been silent most of the ride, finally spoke. "Training's one thing. This is different. You screw up in the sim, you get yelled at. You screw up here, they scrape what's left of you off a roof."

"Helpful," Cal muttered.

"Sib's got a point," Jmeli said, stretching out. "You have about five seconds from jump to stabilization, and if you don't correct your descent, you're eating concrete at terminal velocity. You've got the gear, yeah? Grapple system, impact dampeners?"

Cal nodded. "Yeah, all set."

"Then don't overthink it," Sib said. "Trust your instincts. The biggest mistake people make is fighting the fall. Let the momentum carry you, then use the grapple at the last moment to slow your landing. If you hesitate, you'll either pull too late and crater, or too early and leave yourself a sitting target."

"And keep your legs loose," Nac added. "Lock up and you'll break something."

Jmeli smirked. "Or worse. We had a guy on a drop about a year ago, first mission. Poor bastard panicked and tried to brace himself mid-air. He locked his legs so hard he shattered both knees on landing. Didn't even make it to the fight."

Cal grimaced. "That supposed to make me feel better?"

"Nope," Jmeli said cheerfully. "Just making sure you don't do the same thing."

"Fafa'll grab you if you really screw it up," Bandit called from the cockpit. "But I'd rather not test that theory."

Fafa, ever silent, gave Cal a small, knowing glance but didn't say a word. The message was clear—don't make me have to come back save you.

The comms crackled, Bandit's voice cutting in. "One minute to drop. Get your gear set."

The energy in the flyer shifted. The joking stopped. Harnesses clicked, safeties disengaged, movements becoming precise and practiced. Cal tightened his straps, his heart hammering as the back ramp began to lower, revealing the black void outside.

The ruins stretched below, barely illuminated by the weak moonlight. The wind screamed against the flyer's frame; the ground rushing toward them.

Bandit's team sprang into action. The Flyers weren't just dropping them off—they were guiding them down. Their jet packs activated with a low hum, stabilizing their descent as they moved into position. The War Angels didn't have the luxury of thrusters in their armor. That meant they needed the Flyers to bring them in close before letting them drop.

"Fafa, take Cal and Grassie!" Bandit ordered over the comms.

Fafa gave a single nod before gripping Cal's harness with one arm and hooking Grassie under the other like it was nothing. He didn't hesitate. The moment the War Angels stepped off the ramp, the Flyers dove with them.

For a brief second, the sensation of freefall crushed Cal's breath from his lungs. Then he felt the jolt—Fafa adjusting mid-air, redirecting their trajectory as they dropped in controlled synchronization.

He looked over and saw Bandit, who was holding Darya's gun as he flew them towards the drop zone. Daryas held on with one arm dangling below it, purple glow of her armor making a streak through the sky, seemingly unbothered by the distance of empty space between her and the ground. Below them, the ruins expanded in sharp clarity, jagged metal, collapsed walls, and eerie, empty streets. Everything was too still.

"Stay loose!" Jmeli's voice crackled in his ear. "If you fight the descent, you'll just make it harder!"

Cal forced himself to relax his muscles as Fafa guided them downward. It was strange, unnatural, trusting someone else with his landing. His instincts screamed at him to brace, but he followed Sib's earlier advice—don't fight it.

As they neared the ground, Fafa gave a slight push, releasing Cal and Grassie at just the right moment. Cal hit the dirt, rolling once, momentum carrying him forward before he came to a steady crouch. Grassie landed beside him with the grace of someone who had done this more times than she could count.

Above, the Flyers peeled away, their thrusters flaring as they shot back toward the retreating transport. The mission was fully in the hands of the War Angels now.

The moment the roar of the Flyers' engines faded, silence settled over the ruins. A silence too deep, too unnatural.

Daryas scanned their surroundings, her rifle at the ready. "We regroup, check gear, and then move. We stick to the plan."

No one objected, but Cal could feel the weight of unspoken tension hanging between them. Smokey was the first to voice it.

"Alright," he said, adjusting his rifle, "now that we're here, maybe someone wants to explain why the hell this really got approved."

Cal froze, his hand tightening around his weapon. The others turned to face him and Daryas, expectant.

Cab crossed her arms. "Yeah, no offense, but this mission stinks. We've done recon and salvage before, but this? There's no real extraction plan, no backup. It's a suicide run unless someone at command thinks we'll find something worth dying for."

"And command doesn't care about salvage ops this much," Smokey added. "Not unless there's another reason." His gaze locked onto Cal. "So tell me—what aren't we being told?"

Cal exhaled slowly, feeling the scrutiny settle on him like a physical weight. He started to speak, but Smokey cut him off before he could get the words out.

"Actually?" Smokey's voice was sharp. "Save it. You're not even a Vanguard. If someone's explaining, it's her." He jabbed a finger toward Daryas.

Daryas shot him a warning look. "Smokey—"

"No," he snapped. "We're a team. And teams don't keep secrets from each other. So tell us what's really going on, or we turn around and walk right back."

A tense silence stretched between them.

Daryas exhaled sharply, the sound muffled inside her helmet. "We were ordered to find salvage. That part's true. But we have another objective—one we weren't exactly ready to share. Something command wouldn't approve of if they knew why we wanted it."

Smokey scoffed. "That's not exactly helping your case. Try again."

Daryas squared her shoulders. "We had to keep it quiet because if this mission got flagged for the wrong reasons, it wouldn't have been approved. We needed to be here, and we couldn't risk someone shutting it down before we got on the ground."

Cab let out a short, bitter laugh. "So that's why we got sent in alone. You planned it that way."

"We're War Angels. This is what we do," Rich said, voice calm. "And if Daryas said it had to be done this way, then that's enough for me."

Smokey shook his head. "Yeah? Well, it's not enough for me." He turned to Cal, narrowing his eyes. "And what about him? Why is he here?"

Daryas took a step forward. "Because I trust him."

Smokey let out a sharp breath through his nose, clearly holding back more words. "Yeah, well, I don't."

Cab looked between them. "So what is it? Why are we really here?"

Daryas hesitated. "We're looking for a command level decryption key."

""A what?" Smokey's mood darkened. "And that's just coming up now? We're in the middle of enemy territory, with no support, and now we're learning we're not even here for what we were told?"

He took a step forward, gesturing sharply at Daryas. "Does Commander Varek even know about this? Or are you just deciding to make us all insubordinate without telling us?"

Daryas straightened, her voice measured. "Varek approved this mission. He knows we're here."

"Yeah? And does he know why?" Smokey shot back. "Because if you're keeping this from us, what's stopping you from keeping it from him, too?"

Cal clenched his jaw, stepping in. "Smokey, that's not—"

Smokey cut him off, his voice cold. "Shut up. You're not a Vanguard. You don't get a say in this. You're barely even a soldier. You ask me, you don't even belong to be here. You're a miner. You should be back at base, digging up the shit that makes us roll. But here you are, career decisions for all of us. No, not even that, life and death decisions. We're risking our necks to get a command level encryption key?" Smokey kicked a rock and sent it flying. "I should drop you where you stand right now and bring back your rifle as a trophy."

Tension snapped through the group like a live wire. Daryas lifted a hand between them, her voice firm but calm. "Enough.

This mission was greenlit. But what we're looking for? That had to stay between us until we got here. We had to be sure."

"Sure of what?" Cab asked, her voice tight. "That we wouldn't back out? That we wouldn't refuse to follow orders? We've bled for this squad, and you didn't think we deserved to know?"

Rich, quiet until now, spoke, his voice level. "Would it have changed anything? We're here now. The mission hasn't changed."

Smokey let out a bitter laugh. "Maybe not for you. But now I know I can't trust them. And trust is what keeps us alive."

Daryas met his gaze. "I made the call. If you want to be angry at someone, be angry at me. But we're here now. And we finish what we started."

Smokey exhaled sharply, shaking his head. "Yeah. We finish it. But after that? We're gonna have words."

He stalked ahead, leaving the others behind. The team was still together, but something had cracked. And it was Cal's fault.

"If we had told you before, you would have had the same reaction you're having now," Daryas said. "And we couldn't risk that."

"Risk? Risk?" Smokey shook his head, stepping back. "You don't get to make that call for us. We trust you, Daryas. At least, I did. But you don't get to just decide when we know the truth."

Rich interjected cutting him off, "Would you have come if she told you?"

Smokey hesitated. "That's not the point."

"It is," Grassie said, her tone softer. "You're mad because you feel left out. I get it. But we trust her. And if she thought it was the right call to wait, then it was."

Cab shook her head, arms still crossed. "I don't like it. But we're here now. So we finish what we started."

Smokey took a long breath before finally nodding. "Fine. I'm not happy about it. And I don't trust Cal. But I'll follow Daryas. Just don't ever pull this crap again. And we're still gonna have words."

Daryas met his gaze. "I won't."

The moment passed, the tension settling into something unsteady but stable.

Daryas turned back to the ruins. "We move in. Keep quiet, keep low. Let's find what we came for."

The War Angels moved forward. Smokey still moved like he was pissed. But they had a mission to complete.

Chapter 19 – Dead Men's Secrets

The War Angels moved through the ruined stronghold in silence, their boots crunching over debris and dust. Something was wrong here.

The air inside the facility was still, stagnant, as if the place itself had been abandoned for centuries instead of months. The dim emergency lighting cast long, eerie shadows, flickering intermittently along the rusting walls. A hollow emptiness hung in the air, the kind that sent a primal warning through the senses—this place was dead, but something had killed it.

Cal adjusted his rifle, his gloved fingers tightening around the grip. He had seen dozens of abandoned strongholds before, but this felt... different. There was no sign of battle, no bullet-ridden walls or spent energy cells. The metal surfaces were coated in layers of dust and grime, untouched, as if no one had ever tried to reclaim what was left.

Cab moved ahead, her steps slow and deliberate, stopping at a collapsed doorway. She knelt, brushing away debris and revealing a skeletal hand, the bones bleached from time but still perfectly intact.

"This doesn't make sense," she muttered, brushing dirt off the remains. "If the infected overran this place, where are the turned?"

Smokey stood nearby, his grip tightening on his rifle. "This wasn't the infected. Something else did this."

Rich scanned the area, his helmeted head turning methodically. "Spread out. Let's see what we're dealing with."

Grassie moved up next to Cal, her voice lower than usual. "This place feels wrong."

Cal nodded, swallowing the unease creeping up his spine. Something had wiped this base clean, but it hadn't been the infected. And that meant whatever had done this was calculated—efficient. The lack of decay, the intact skeletons, the lack of turned... It wasn't just unsettling. It was impossible.

Cal had expected signs of an infection-driven massacre—bloodstains, signs of struggle, barricades overrun. Instead, the skeletal remains of Coalition soldiers and personnel lay where they had fallen, untouched, their bones eerily intact. The infected always turned their victims, but these people hadn't turned. They had died where they stood.

Cab knelt beside a fallen soldier, brushing dirt off the remains. "This doesn't make sense. If the infected overran this place, where are the turned?"

Smokey's grip tightened on his rifle. "This wasn't the infected. Something else did this."

Rich turned, scanning the area. "Spread out. Let's see what we're dealing with."

As they pushed deeper into the facility, the signs of an organized collapse became clearer. Notes scrawled hastily onto walls, warning of something inside the base, not outside. Broken-down doors with marks from energy weapons, not claws or teeth. Voice recorders left behind with unfinished messages.

Cal picked up a small recording device from a desk, its casing cracked. He pressed play, and the team froze as a panicked voice filled the air.

"They're inside. I don't know how, but they're inside. Command says to hold position, but—oh God, they're coming. We locked the—"

The audio cut off abruptly.

Grassie shifted uncomfortably. "That's not the usual 'we're being overrun' message."

"No," Daryas agreed. "It's not."

Cal exhaled sharply, his gaze shifting from the recorder to the skeletal remains around them. They were missing something. The pieces didn't fit. "If this wasn't the infected, then what the hell could've done this? Coalition deserters? Some rogue faction we've never heard of?"

Smokey shook his head, scanning the walls with narrowed eyes. "Not likely. If it was another faction, there'd be signs of occupation—makeshift camps, different markings, scavenged supplies. This place wasn't taken. It was erased."

"What if they turned on each other?" Grassie suggested. "Panic spreads fast in a fall. Could've been an internal breakdown. Officers giving bad orders, people turning on command, maybe even execution squads."

Cab frowned. "No. That doesn't explain the lack of survivors. If it was a mutiny, some of them would've made it out. But no one came back here. No Coalition clean-up crews, no raiders. Nothing."

Rich let out a slow breath. "Which means whatever did this... it didn't leave witnesses."

The thought made the air feel heavier, pressing in around them like the ruins themselves were listening.

Cal's fingers tightened around his rifle. He looked back down at the hastily scrawled warnings on the walls. They're inside. Do not engage. Run.

Daryas straightened. "We're wasting time. If we're going to figure this out, we need to move deeper. Whatever happened here, command will have the answers."

The deeper they went, the more restricted the base became. Hallways narrowed, defensive barriers were still in place, untouched since the fall. When they finally reached a reinforced security checkpoint, the blast doors were sealed tight. Their panels were dark, lifeless. The doors had been shut before the facility went silent—locked from the inside.

Cal ran a gloved hand over the console. "This was locked before the collapse. Someone didn't want anything getting in."

"Or out," Grassie muttered.

Smokey stepped back, staring at the solid metal. "So what's the play? We blasting through?"

Rich shook his head. "Not unless we want to bring the whole place down on us."

Daryas exhaled, scanning the room. "Look for an alternate route. These places always had emergency access points. Maintenance tunnels, ventilation systems—anything."

After several minutes of searching, Grassie called out from across the corridor. "Got something. Looks like an old maintenance shaft. Cramped, but it might get us past the lockdown."

Cab frowned. "We're really gonna crawl through that?"

"You got a better idea?" Grassie shot back.

With some grudging agreement, they started clearing debris. It took nearly half an hour of shifting rubble and cutting through rusted plating before they managed to pry open an access point big enough to crawl through. The tunnel beyond was dark, stale air hanging thick inside.

Daryas went in first, moving cautiously. One by one, they followed, pushing through the tight, claustrophobic space, their breath loud in the silence. The tunnel twisted downward, leading into another sealed corridor—one that had been bypassed completely when the base was abandoned.

They emerged into a long corridor, the air thick with the stale scent of dust and decay. The overhead lights were dim, some flickering weakly, casting jittering shadows against the metal walls. Every footstep echoed, a hollow sound in the empty facility.

Daryas motioned forward, her voice quieter now. "Stay sharp. We're getting close."

As they rounded the last corner Cal spotted something slumped up against the wall.

A body.

At first glance, it looked like any other fallen soldier in the stronghold, but something was different. The armor—heavier plating, reinforced joints—wasn't standard Coalition issue. He crouched down, brushing dust from the shoulder plate, and felt his stomach tighten at the unmistakable insignia.

"Vanguard," he whispered.

The realization sank in slowly, like ice creeping up his spine. He had never seen a dead Vanguard before.

The others gathered around, but no one spoke at first. The silence stretched, heavy and unnatural, as if the weight of what they were seeing hadn't fully settled yet. Grassie let out a low whistle, but it wasn't her usual playful tone—it was quiet, almost reverent. "That's... not something you see every day."

Cal swallowed hard, his stomach twisting. Seeing fallen soldiers was one thing. Seeing them—the Vanguard—dead, hollowed out in their armor, was another. He had spent his life looking up to them, imagining them as unstoppable. Unbreakable. And yet, here they were, nothing but remnants, their power stripped away, their trexium cores completely drained.

Smokey exhaled, his fingers drumming against his rifle. "What the hell kills a Vanguard and walks away?"

Cab shook her head, her expression grim. "Nothing that we've ever seen before. A Grave Titan maybe. But this wasn't a Grave Titan."

Smokey's jaw tensed before asking again. "Then what the hell killed him?"

Then Rich's voice, quiet but firm. "It's not just one."

Cal looked up, following Rich's gaze to a cluster of bodies further down the corridor. Four more figures, slumped in what must have been their final formation. Their armor looked intact at first glance, but something was off.

Cab knelt beside one, reaching out carefully. When her fingers brushed against the shoulder plate, the armor collapsed inward, hollow.

"They're just skeletons inside," she murmured. "Their trexium reserves are completely depleted."

Cal's pulse pounded in his ears. He had idolized the Vanguard, spent his life looking up to them. They weren't supposed to die like this. Not drained, not left to rot in silence.

Daryas exhaled. "Whatever they were fighting, it took everything they had. And it still wasn't enough."

"They were flyers too. Imagine, having all that training to fight in the sky, and then dying here," Cab shuddered.

The War Angels stood in silence before the ruined Vanguard team, the weight of the moment settling over them like a thick fog. Five Vanguard, drained of power, their armor nothing more than empty husks. The strongest warriors the Coalition had ever trained, brought down by something no one understood.

Cal swallowed, forcing himself to look away. He had never truly considered that Vanguards could die like this. It was different from seeing fallen soldiers, different from even losing his parents. This was a reminder that no one was invincible.

Daryas took a slow breath. "We keep moving."

She stepped past the skeletal remains and motioned toward the door at the end of the hall. The entrance to the command center.

"Locked?" Smokey asked.

Rich moved up, inspecting the panel. He tapped at the dark screen, his fingers skimming over the reinforced metal, but there was no response. "Dead system. The security locks engaged before power was lost."

"Figures," Cab muttered. "How do we get through?"

Grassie moved beside her, peering at the door's seams. "These locks weren't designed to be breached easily. We'd need a Coalition access code to override it."

Cal exhaled sharply, stepping back. "Or a manual override. There's got to be something. A failsafe in case command ever needed to force their way in."

Daryas looked toward the bodies again. "If anyone had the authority to force their way inside, it would've been the Vanguard."

Smokey scowled. "You're suggesting we search them?"

"I'm suggesting we do what we have to," she shot back. "Help me move them."

There was no hesitation after that. One by one, they checked the fallen, peeling back damaged plating, searching for anything that could give them access. Each moment stretched, the sound of shifting armor and quiet breathing filling the silence.

Cal's hands shook slightly as he searched the last soldier, but then his fingers brushed something hard, wedged beneath the armored plating of the Vanguard's wrist.

"Got something," he said.

He pulled it free—a small, thin keycard, its edges singed but still intact. A Coalition base-level override key.

Daryas took it from him, inspecting the markings before stepping toward the door. "Let's hope it still works."

She swiped the keycard. A sharp beep filled the air, followed by the clunk of magnetic locks disengaging. The door hissed open slightly before stopping, jammed halfway from months of neglect. Dust billowed into the air, the scent of decay rolling out to meet them.

Smokey shoved his shoulder into the door, grunting as he pushed. "Give me a hand."

Rich joined him, their combined strength forcing the heavy metal apart. The gap widened just enough for them to slip through.

Inside, the war room was frozen in time.

Screens that had once displayed battle formations and active operations now flickered weakly, their displays filled with static. The large circular command table sat untouched, layers of dust clinging to its surface. Paperwork, shattered data pads, and discarded weaponry were scattered across the floor.

And at the center of the room, slumped over his desk, was the base commander's decayed body.

Cab stepped forward cautiously. "Looks like he died at his post."

The team spread out, searching through the scattered remains of the war room. Papers crumbled under their boots, dust swirling with every step. Broken monitors flickered with dying energy, their screens frozen on outdated tactical readouts.

"There's gotta be something in here," Smokey muttered, flipping over a toppled chair. "Command wouldn't just sit here waiting to die. They were trying to do something."

Cal moved cautiously around the room, his eyes scanning for anything that stood out. His gaze drifted toward the commander's skeletal remains, hunched over his desk, decayed fingers still curled as if holding something in place.

But then he noticed something else—the angle of his arm.

The bones of his outstretched hand pointed stiffly toward the far side of the room, where an old storage cabinet lay half-cracked open, its contents hidden in shadow.

"He was pointing to something," Cal said, his voice hushed.

Daryas turned toward him, following his gaze. "Then let's find out what it was."

They moved quickly, pushing aside scattered debris to pry the cabinet fully open. Inside, buried beneath layers of old reports and rusted ammunition casings, was a data core—the same kind Cal had seen before. This was the same kind of object he saw in Corvin's case onboard the airship when the stronghold was being moved, before they had been attacked by zombie flyers.

His breath caught as he reached in and pulled it free, feeling the weight of it in his hands. The team gathered around, the room eerily silent.

"This is it," he murmured.

Daryas stepped up beside him, her voice low. "We need to see what's inside, but we can't even open it yet."

Cal turned the data core over in his hands. The casing was heavier than he expected, reinforced. It wasn't just a data drive—it was something more. "It's locked. Probably requires an authentication key."

"Which we don't have," Smokey muttered. He kicked at a fallen data pad, frustration evident in his posture. "So now what? We hit a dead end?"

Cal frowned, his gaze shifting back to the commander's skeletal form. Something still wasn't right. The body was slumped over, bones wrapped in the remnants of a Coalition officer's uniform, but his hand... his hand wasn't just resting on the desk. It was clenched.

A chill ran down Cal's spine. He stepped closer, reaching out. The bones shifted slightly as he pried open the decayed fingers.

Something small and metallic dropped onto the desk with a faint clink. A data chip.

"Got something," Cal said, picking it up. The edges were worn, but the markings matched the encryption locks on the core. This was it—the key to whatever was inside.

Daryas took a sharp breath. "That's how we open it. Get power to a terminal, now."

Smokey pulled a trexium core from his belt, rolling it in his palm before slotting it into the power receptacle on a hopefully-still-functioning console. The monitor hummed to life, dim but operational.

Cal took a breath, inserted his own data chip, with the encrypted data and watched as the screen began to load.

Just as he was about to insert the decryption key, the monitor flickered.

Commander Varek's face appeared on the screen.

Chapter 20 – The Purge and the Price

Cal's breath caught in his throat as Varek's face flickered to life on the dim screen. The grainy transmission carried a faint static hum, but the image was clear enough to make out every line of exhaustion on the commander's face.

Varek exhaled slowly, as if bracing himself. "I was hoping Corvin was wrong," he said at last. "That you hadn't come this far. But now I see you have. Tell me, where are the War Angels?"

Cal felt a dozen emotions at once—anger, betrayal, confusion—but above all, he wanted answers. His hands curled into fists at his sides as he stepped closer to the monitor. The War Angels were frozen, listening in silence. Varek didn't know they were there.

Cal stared at the screen, his breath slow, steadying himself. Varek had stopped him from accessing the data, stopped him from seeing the truth for himself. That meant whatever was on that drive was dangerous—too dangerous for them to see.

Cal stepped forward, keeping his voice measured. "The War Angels are outside. They can't hear any of this. Just me."

Varek's expression remained unreadable, but there was a slight shift—a calculation, a weighing of options.

"And Daryas?" Varek asked, his tone almost casual. "How much does she know?"

Cal hesitated just for a second before answering. "Nothing. I couldn't risk anyone knowing. She thought I was after something, but she didn't know what."

It was a lie. A clean one. A necessary one.

Varek studied him for a moment, then sighed. "I wanted better for you, Cal. I saw your potential, the way you fought, the way you questioned things. If you had been patient, if you had trusted the system, I could have given you so much more. But instead, you're standing here, demanding answers you aren't ready to hear."

Cal's jaw tightened. "Then explain it to me. Why keep the truth from us? Why let us fight and die for something that no one understands?"

Varek shook his head. "Because *you* don't understand yet. Because if you did, you wouldn't be fighting me. You'd be standing beside me."

"What was so important that you couldn't risk me seeing it?"

Varek exhaled, shaking his head slightly. "It's not about what's on the drive, Cal. It's about what you think you're looking for. Answers? A way to fix all of this? To undo what's already been set in motion? You won't find that here. You're looking at the past. You don't even realize that I'm offering you the future."

Cal's jaw tightened. "Then tell me. No more excuses, no more half-truths. If you really think you're right, then tell me everything." There was too much he didn't understand, too many questions building inside him. He took a step forward, watching Varek's expression, searching for any trace of hesitation.

Varek's expression didn't change. He sighed, his gaze drifting for a moment, as if recalling something long past. "Because, Cal, I was you once. A long time ago. A farm boy, scraping by, just another nameless recruit until I was pulled up into something greater. And I believed—truly believed—that I was fighting for a better future. That's what I saw in you. A leader. Someone who could have been part of it, if only you had been patient."

Cal's stomach twisted. "Part of what?"

Varek's gaze sharpened, his tone grew almost manic. "Peace, Cal. True peace. Not the illusion of stability, not the cycles of war that leave us clawing for survival every few months. Real order. The kind that can't be challenged. The kind that no one can undo!"

Cal's breath came faster now. "You're talking about control. You mean a world where no one can resist. A world where the virus—"

"—isn't a plague," Varek interrupted. "It's a tool. A tool that got out of control, yes. But we can't change that and it doesn't mean it can't still serve its purpose. The Coalition system was never just about survival. It was about finding a way to make war impossible. If we can control the infected, then what's stopping us from controlling everything else? What's stopping us from ensuring no more rebellions, no more uprisings, no more bloodshed?"

Cal swallowed hard, forcing himself to push past the nausea creeping up his throat. "Start from the beginning, Varek. How did it all start? The virus, the Coalition, the war—explain it all. Help me understand," Cal switched to a tone of pleading. Maybe if Varek thought Cal could be convinced Varek would reveal more.

Varek sighed, his shoulders rising and falling with the weight of what he was about to say. "The virus wasn't a mistake, Cal. It was designed. Engineered. Not to kill indiscriminately, but to control. It was meant to reshape warfare itself—an invisible leash to turn enemies into tools, soldiers into something more obedient. The first trials were... promising. Until it spread beyond containment. Until we realized we had made something we couldn't reverse."

Cal's grip on the edge of the console tightened. "So, what? You just kept going? You didn't stop to think maybe this was a line you shouldn't cross?"

Varek shook his head. "There was no turning back. Once we understood that even the infected could be guided, manipulated, we saw the potential. Not just as weapons, but as a means to bring true, lasting order. Imagine a world where war wasn't decided by who had the bigger guns, but by who controlled the minds of their enemies.

"But control isn't enough if it can be undone," Varek continued. "That's when the real work began. We needed a space where we could not only refine the virus but see how humanity reacted to it. If we were to design a perfect system, we needed to know every possible countermeasure before it was ever deployed. That's when the testing ground was built—massive, enclosed, self-sustaining. A world within a world."

Cal's breath came short. "They...you...whoever started this... built this? The whole valley? All of the other valleys? It's not just remnants of the past?"

Varek nodded, his expression hardening. "We gathered what we could of humanity and brought them here, inside the experiment. Every three months, conditions shift—new threats, new mutations, new environments. Desert climates, frozen wastelands, infection speeds, spread mechanisms—all of it designed to force adaptation. To see what worked. To see how humans fought back, how they resisted, and then to ensure that resistance could be neutralized. Every move you've made, every battle you've fought, has been another test. Another piece of data to refine the system. You were never just surviving, Cal. You were being studied.

"And that's why the purge exists," Varek continued, his pace quickening again. "Every stronghold that falls, every settlement that collapses—it's not left behind. It's wiped clean. The purge doesn't just destroy the infected, it eliminates everything artificial. Every structure, every piece of tech, every sign that another group of survivors came before you. Only natural resources remain— ruins, forests, mountains. It keeps the illusion intact. It keeps the test pure. We cannot afford for test subjects to recognize they are not the first. With enough trexium at our disposal, we can turn that energy to cleansing the land of all traces of human existence."

"The missing shipment. You steal from the coalitions who mine it to wipe out their history! That's why we've never found old bases intact. Why every valley looks untouched before we settle in. You make sure we never see the remnants of the people who came before us."

Varek nodded. "If a single survivor from an erased Coalition were to stumble into an active one, it could unravel centuries of research. That can't be allowed to happen. Every iteration must start from the same conditions, without outside contamination. That is how we perfect control."

He began pacing as he explained.

"Agents within every coalition monitor and coordinate information. They communicate, they run the experiment. And when a worthy member of the test group arises, they find a way to promote them. To encourage them in their growth, just as we did with you. Just as was done with me before."

Cal blinked, his body tensing. "Encourage me? What the hell are you talking about?"

Varek stopped pacing, his gaze sharp. "You think you're just naturally gifted? That you were born this way? That your mind is simply... different? No, Cal. You were made this way."

The words sent a cold shock through him.

"You're lying."

Varek smirked. "Am I? Think about it. The way you absorb information. The way you process patterns before others even see them. The way your mind pulls at threads, unraveling things you were never meant to question."

Cal's stomach twisted. "That doesn't mean anything. Some people are just—"

"No," Varek cut him off. "We designed you to be what you are. We needed a mind that could adapt, that could think beyond the standard parameters. Just as we needed soldiers, tacticians, leaders—each generation better than the last."

Cal's breath came in short, uneven bursts. "That's insane."

"Is it?" Varek tilted his head, studying him. "We have the ability to mutate viruses, to shape the very fabric of biology itself. You think we wouldn't apply that to something as controllable as the human genome? You were altered before you were even born, your DNA re-sequenced to enhance intelligence, adaptability, and instinct. You are living proof that we can create a better breed of leadership."

"No," Cal muttered, shaking his head. His voice wavered. "My parents—"

"Never knew," Varek said smoothly. "They were part of the program without realizing it, selected for genetic compatibility. You were an investment from the moment of conception."

The world tilted. Cal clenched his fists. "You call that progress? You call that choice?"

Varek's expression didn't change. "I call it survival. You are proof that we can guide evolution itself, that we can forge something greater. Imagine a world where war wasn't decided by who had the bigger guns, but by who controlled the minds of their enemies."

Cal's stomach turned violently. "You call that peace? That's not order. That's slavery."

Varek's expression darkened. "No, Cal. That's the only way forward. Tell me, how many strongholds have you seen fall? And not just at the hands of the infected, but because they hated each other? Fellow survivors? How many have been wiped off the map, their people slaughtered? We've lived in a world of endless war. This was the only way to stop it. The only way to make sure no one ever needed to fight again."

"You justify this by calling it peace?" he spat. "You're talking about enslaving entire populations. You're talking about enslaving everyone!"

Varek shook his head. "No. I'm talking about the end of chaos. The end of suffering. I see myself in you, Cal. That same fire, that same belief in something greater. If you had been patient—if you had waited—I could have given you everything. The same way my commander gave me everything. He pulled me up from the dirt, from a life that would've amounted to nothing. I was given purpose. You could have had the same."

Cal's stomach twisted, but he didn't let Varek control the conversation. He took a breath, forcing his tone to stay measured. "What's outside, Varek? What's beyond the test? Beyond the mountains? What's left?"

Varek's gaze darkened, the flicker of an old wound crossing his face. "Nothing." He let the word settle before he continued. "Centuries of war destroyed everything outside. Factions rose and fell, each one convinced they could do it better than the last, each one tearing civilization apart piece by piece. This world—our world—is the last hope humanity has. And the only thing keeping it from collapsing again is the work we've done here."

Cal's pulse quickened. "You don't know that. Maybe there are survivors. Maybe there's something out there—"

"There isn't," Varek interrupted, his voice cold. "We know because we sent expeditions. All of them came back with the same report. What remains beyond these walls is nothing but ruin, an endless wasteland where no one lives. What little life we found was small. Barely and plants, twisted, malformed animals. And if humanity were to reemerge, if we were to let them, history would repeat itself. Again and again. Just as it always has."

Cal's fists clenched. "So instead of giving people a chance to rebuild, you keep them caged."

Varek shook his head. "I—no we, the base commanders and agents of the experiment, keep them alive. We learned the truth long ago—freedom is what nearly wiped us out. Every time humanity is given the choice, they splinter into factions, divide into ideologies, and go to war. That's why this must continue. Because if the test ends, if the control is lost, then so is the last hope of our species."

Varek's tone softened, almost pleading now. "Don't you see, Cal? The virus isn't our enemy. It's our only chance. If we control it, if we refine it, we can ensure there's never another war. Peace through order. Through fear of what we could unleash. No one would ever rise against authority again. There would be no ability to."

Cal's stomach churned as realization settled in. "So that's it. You'd rather rule over ruins than risk letting people choose for themselves."

Cal clenched his fists. He had admired Varek. Trusted him. And now, every word out of his mouth was a lie.

"And the others?" Cal asked, voice sharp. "The War Angels? What happens to them?"

Varek's expression became one of consideration before he began, slowly at first. "If what you've said is true then, assuming they survive, they'll always have a home here. They've been my best soldiers. My most loyal. I'd hate to lose them. But to save the work that's been going on for generations, they are a small enough sacrifice. We'll scout the area afterwards. If they're there, we'll bring them home. If they're not, then that's an... unfortunate... side effect."

Cal felt his blood run cold.

Cal's breath came in sharp, uneven gasps. "You're just going to abandon them? After everything?"

Another voice answered.

Corvin.

The scientist stepped into the frame, his expression devoid of anything resembling humanity. There was no anger, no triumph—just calculated efficiency, like he was confirming the results of an experiment. A test that had run its course.

"A purge has been initiated," Corvin stated, his voice smooth, unaffected. "We can't take any risks. The data you've uncovered is dangerous in the wrong hands. Misguided individuals could start asking the wrong questions. And we can't have that. If the War Angels are indeed not with you, they should see the purge begin and escape. If they don't, then there's nothing anyone can do for them now."

Cal's stomach dropped. "You're wiping everything?"

Corvin's head tilted slightly, almost curious. "Of course. You didn't think we'd let an anomaly like this continue, did you? Every failed recruit before you was erased. You will be no different. It's the only way to maintain the purity of the test."

Cal inhaled sharply. "You son of a—"

A deep, distant rumble shook the facility, followed by a low, inhuman howl.

Corvin glanced toward something off-screen, then smiled faintly. "Don't run Cal. There's no way for you to survive. Embrace this as the outcome of your incessant need for answers and your misguided sense of morality. The purge is charging, it will be over soon."

The monitor went black, the last traces of Corvin's smug expression vanishing into darkness. Then the alarms blared, their shrill tones cutting through the silence like a blade.

Cal didn't hesitate. He turned sharply on his heel, his voice rising above the sudden chaos. "Move! Now!"

The War Angels didn't need to be told twice. Boots thundered against metal as they ran, tearing out of the command center.

The entire stronghold seemed to groan as if waking up from a long sleep, but it wasn't waking—it was dying. The lights flickered wildly, distant explosions rattling the walls. And then came the sound no one wanted to hear.

Gunfire. Controlled, precise gunfire.

Daryas cursed. "It's not just the purge. We've got incoming!"

"Who?" Grassie snapped, already pulling her rifle into firing position.

"Not who," Cab muttered, adjusting her stance. "What."

The first shots slammed into the wall beside them. Too precise. Too coordinated. Not the wild, chaotic fire of desperate raiders or the mindless swipes of the infected. This was something else.

Then they saw them.

Figures moved in the dim corridors ahead—infected, but not like any they'd faced before. Their forms were grotesque, mutated beyond recognition, but their eyes were sharp. Focused. And worse—they held weapons. Not just crude scavenged tools, but fully functioning firearms.

They weren't just mindlessly attacking.

They were hunting.

Smokey fired first, dropping the lead creature with a headshot. It didn't stagger. It fell back in a controlled motion, like a soldier bracing from recoil.

"That's not normal," he growled.

Daryas didn't stop moving. "We fight through! Keep moving!"

The War Angels pushed forward, blasting through the infected soldiers, but every gain they made was short-lived. For every enemy they put down, more appeared. They weren't retreating. They were advancing, driving them back, forcing them into tighter spaces.

Rich fired down a hallway, his shots precise. "They're corralling us."

"No shit!" Smokey barked, throwing a grenade back toward the enemy before ducking behind a broken console.

The explosion rocked the corridor, but when the smoke cleared, the infected were still moving, reorganizing, adapting.

Then, from above them, a new threat emerged, an airship the size of which none of them had ever seen blocked out the sky. A pink glow began to emanate from an opening on its under side.

"That has to be the Purge!" Cal yelled. "Move, move!"

Cal's mind raced. The purge would wipe everything. Everything man made and artificial. They would be erased, not even Vanguard armor could save them.

Think, think!

It wouldn't touch the trexium mines! If it did, it could destabilize the entire ore vein and wipe out more than just this stronghold site. Trexium explosions were highly energetic. Besides, there would be no power for the next phase of the experiment or the next wave of survivors.

"We go for the mines!" he shouted. "It's our only shot!"

They ran, dodging gunfire and suppressing the horde behind them as they sprinted toward the lower levels. The walls trembled with the force of the coming purge, the temperature rising as energy built up around them.

The entrance to the mines came into view. A reinforced metal doorway, partially ajar, leading into darkness.

"Inside!" Daryas ordered. One by one, they disappeared into the tunnel. But Cal and Smokey were the last ones in.

Then it happened.

An infected burst from the shadows, raising a rifle—aiming directly at Cal.

There was no time to react.

Smokey moved first.

The shot rang out, hitting him square in the chest. He staggered back, gasping as he collapsed onto one knee.

Cal's world blurred. He didn't think—he just acted. He raised his rifle and fired, dropping the infected attacker in an instant before grabbing Smokey by the shoulders and dragging him inside.

The door slammed shut, and Cal dropped the latch, sealing them below.

A second later, the purge hit.

The ground shook violently, sending tremors through the mine shaft. Dust and rock rained from above. A section of the tunnel collapsed, separating Cal and Smokey from the others.

"No, no, no—" Cal scrambled toward the fallen debris, trying to move it, but it was already settling into place, the weight too much to shift.

"They'll be fine," Smokey rasped from behind him.

Cal turned, kneeling beside him. Smokey's breathing was labored, his chest plate dark with spreading blood from where the shot had found one of the few weak points in the armor.

"You're okay," Cal said, shaking his head. "I'll patch you up. We'll get back to them."

Smokey gave a weak chuckle as he pulled his helmet off. "Don't lie to me, kid. I know when it's bad."

Cal clenched his jaw. "No. Not like this. You're fine. I'll fix this. Just—just stay awake."

Cal tried to scream for Cab but got no reply.

"You know," Smokey said coughing up a small spittle of blood, "She'd kill me if I told you this, but I think it's too late for that. Her name's not Cab. It's Cabbage."

Cal sat stunned. Of all the things for Smokey to say, that was not high on his list of likelihoods or priorities.

"She grew up hauling produce in the trade convoys between strongholds—mostly cabbages. When we found out, we called her the Cabbage Kid. She hated it. Punched someone so hard in the mouth that when the instructor asked who did it, all he could say was 'Cab'. Now? It's all she answers to."

Cal couldn't help but smile at the story.

Smokey's breaths came shallow and ragged, each one a fight. His fingers twitched against the cold rock floor, his body trembling. Cal held onto him, pressing a hand against the wound, but the blood was pooling too fast, seeping through his gloves and coming from under the chest plate.

"Dammit, Smokey, stay with me," Cal muttered, voice cracking. "Just keep breathing. Just a little longer."

Smokey exhaled a shaky, wet breath, a weak chuckle mixed in with the sound of gurgling. "Look at you... giving orders now."

Cal tried to force a smile, but it wouldn't come. "Guess you guys finally rubbed off on me."

Smokey's eyes, barely visible behind his flickering visor, softened. "Listen... what Varek said, about you being...made, or whatever it was. Don't let that get to you. I was wrong about you. About a lot of things. You're okay, Miner. By me, you're okay. No matter how you got here."

Cal shook his head. "No. Don't do that. Don't act like this is over. We're getting out of here. Together."

Smokey let out another pained laugh, but his voice grew weaker. "You always were too damn stubborn. Just... take care of Daryas, alright? She's tougher than she looks, but even she needs someone watching her back."

Cal's vision blurred. "You're going to do it yourself."

Smokey grinned, but it was fleeting, fading as he reached for the clasp on his chest plate. The armor let out a hiss, disengaging as he pulled free a small data chip from within.

His hand, slick with blood, pressed it into Cal's palm. "Access chip. My armor. It's yours now. Just don't... don't scuff it up, Miner."

Cal's fingers curled around it, his breath coming in short gasps. "Smokey, please—"

Smokey smiled, a faint, tired thing. His fingers twitched once, then stilled.

His silver screened visor flickered, then went dark.

And Smokey was gone.

Chapter 21 – The Weight of a Warrior

Cal didn't move.

The silence felt alive, stretching into the empty cavern like it was waiting to swallow him whole. His breaths were shallow, controlled, as if any sudden movement would break the fragile reality of the moment. The weight of the purge still lingered in the air, the distant rumble of destruction now nothing more than a memory.

The silence following the purge was oppressive, pressing in on him from all sides. The world above had been wiped clean, erased by the energy that had surged through the stronghold. But down here, below the destruction, all that remained was stillness.

Smokey's body lay beside him, motionless. The weight of his death sat heavy in the space. The heat from the firefight still clung to Cal's skin, but the mine itself was cold, the air thick with dust from the collapse. He couldn't hear anything from the other side of the rubble—not Cab, not Rich, not Grassie, not Daryas. For the first time since this mission started, he was completely alone.

Cal sat back, his back pressing against the rough stone wall of the mine. He didn't cry. Not yet. His hands were still covered in blood, Smokey's blood, still warm, still fresh. He could still hear his voice—gruff, sarcastic, always ready with a jab. And now? Nothing.

His gaze drifted down to the small data chip clenched in his hand. Smokey's armor access key. It felt impossibly small for something so heavy. His fingers curled around it, gripping it like an anchor, like it might hold back the tide threatening to pull him under. A final act, a final decision—to pass something on. To give Cal a piece of him to carry forward.

A tremor ran through Cal's fingers as he stared at it. This wasn't supposed to happen. They were supposed to make it. They were supposed to walk away from this, even if it meant running. But Smokey hadn't run. He had made a choice-to save Cal.

Cal inhaled sharply, pushing away the grief that clawed at the edge of his mind. Not now. Not yet.

Slowly, methodically, he turned toward Smokey's body. He had to move.

But he didn't—not at first. His muscles resisted, his mind screaming for just another second. Another moment to sit in this space where Smokey still existed, where his body was still warm, where the silence hadn't completely taken him yet. But moments didn't last, and time didn't wait. He had to do this.

He reached out, his hands still shaking as he began the process of removing Smokey's armor. It was heavier than he expected. The plates locked together with reinforced seals, designed to withstand the worst conditions imaginable. Smokey had taken a direct hit, and the armor would have absorbed it—but not at point blank range, and not in that spot, one of the few weak points in the protective layers.

Cal's fingers fumbled at the chest plate's release mechanism. The hiss of depressurization filled the chamber as the plates unlocked, loosening their grip around the lifeless body beneath. The process wasn't quick. Every piece had to be removed carefully, layer by layer. The suit was built for endurance, for battle, and taking it apart was a slow, deliberate effort.

It felt wrong.

Like he was peeling away the last part of Smokey that was still here.

The boots came first, heavy and reinforced with stabilizers for precision movement. Then the leg armor, the gauntlets, the forearm plates—each piece revealing more of the person underneath, until finally, only the chest piece remained. It was the piece that locked everything else in.

Cal hesitated. His hands hovered over the final release, his breath uneven. This wasn't just armor. This was who Smokey was.

But he had given it to him. He had chosen this. It was Smokey's way of telling Cal he was ready. Ready to be a Vanguard.

Swallowing hard, Cal pressed the final release, and the chest plate unlatched. He lifted it away, feeling the weight of it in his arms before setting it down carefully beside him. He reached for the helmet last, pausing only for a moment before sliding it free.

Smokey's face was peaceful. Too peaceful. Cal studied him, searching for something—anything—that made this feel real. It didn't. It felt like a mistake, like he was stuck in a loop where Smokey would open his eyes at any moment, smirk, and call him an idiot for wasting time. But the visor wouldn't flicker back on. The voice wouldn't come. Like he was just resting, like at any moment he would stir and say something snarky about Cal taking too damn long. But he wouldn't. Not ever again.

Cal set the helmet down beside the armor, his hands running over the gear like it might still hold some part of the man who had worn it. He let his fingers linger on the chest plate, tracing the worn edges, the places where battles had left their mark. Every dent, every scratch was a story Smokey would never get to tell.

His throat tightened. He had no words, no prayers, nothing to give but this final act—taking up the weight Smokey had carried before him.

As he lifted the chest plate, his fingers tracing over the deep grooves and scratches, a thought settled into his mind. They had called him Miner from the start. At first, it had been a knock, a tease. He wasn't one of them, just a kid who dug rocks and got lucky.

But somewhere along the way, it had changed. He hadn't noticed it at first, but now, in the silence, it was obvious. They hadn't been mocking him. They had given him his name. Just like Smokey, like Cab, like Not a Chance. It had become a part of him, something he had earned. He had stopped being just Cal a long time ago. Then, finally, he began the slow process of putting it on.

It wasn't just about survival.

It was about carrying him forward and finishing the job as Smokey would have.

The helmet clicked into place, and from that point on, he knew. He wasn't Cal anymore.

He was a member of the Vanguard.

He was a member of the Angels of War.

He was Miner.

Chapter 22 – Reunions and Reckonings

The weight of the armor settled over Miner's shoulders like a ghost pressing into his skin. It wasn't just gear. It was a name, a legacy, and a burden all at once. The moments passed in silence as he sat in the dark of the mines, his breathing steady inside the helmet. It still carried the faintest scent of Smokey—metal, sweat, and something else, something human—but that, too, would fade with time.

Time.

He didn't know how long he had been sitting there; the silence stretching on, unbroken. Then, the distant muffled sounds of movement made him tense. The others.

Miner pushed himself to his feet, adjusting the armor as he moved through the tunnels. The passage that led to where the others were was collapsed, but other routes through the rock were still stable—for now. The passage twisted and narrowed, the walls pressing in before opening into a wider shaft where chunks of rock still crumbled from the ceiling, shaken loose by the purge. The air was thick with dust, making it hard to see, but he could hear something—movement. Voices. Distant, but there.

He followed the sound, his pace quickening despite the weight of the armor. The path sloped downward before curving sharply to the right. Then he saw a faint, flickering glow ahead—emergency lights casting long shadows.

A figure moved, shifting between the beams of red light. Then another. Four of them. Armed. Alert.

His heart clenched. It had to be them.

Miner stepped forward, his movement drawing every set of eyes toward him. He knew what they saw first—the armor, the familiar silhouette. And for one fraction of a second, he saw hope.

"Smokey?" Daryas asked hesitantly.

Then, as he reached up and unlocked the helmet seal, the hiss of depressurization filled the chamber before he pulled it free. He met their eyes, his face covered in grime, exhaustion etched into every line.

"No," Miner said, his voice quieter than he intended. "It's me."

A beat of silence. Then realization crashed over them like a tidal wave.

"Cal! How did you—" Daryas started.

"Miner." Cal said, firmly, but kindly. The four of them stood, staring at him with a strange kind of understanding before Daryas nodded. They knew and would never call him Cal again.

"Smokey's gone," Miner said, forcing the words past the tightness in his throat. "He stepped in front of a bullet for me. Told me to take his armor. I tried, but I can't do anything."

Cab inhaled sharply, turning her head, pressing her lips together like she could physically stop herself from reacting. But her clenched fists gave her away.

Rich exhaled through his nose, slow and steady, but he said nothing.

Grassie was the first to move. She stepped forward, reaching up to press a hand against the chest plate, her fingers tracing the edges of the scratches and dents. Her voice was soft when she spoke. "He told you to take it?"

Miner nodded. "His last words."

Daryas swallowed, her jaw tightening as she took a step forward. But instead of speaking, she looked at him for a long moment. Then she exhaled, steadying herself. "Then we carry him with us."

When they emerged onto the surface, the stronghold was gone.

There was nothing. No ruins, no broken walls, no shattered barricades. Not even bones. The purge had wiped it completely clean, stripping away every trace that people had ever lived and died here. The ground was eerily smooth, untouched, as if the land had never known war or suffering. Only a single gaping hole leading down into the mines remained—a scar in the earth marking the only evidence that something had once stood here.

Miner felt his stomach twist. This was worse than fire. Worse than destruction. Fire left ruins, gave proof that something had existed. This was sterility. This was erasure.

Daryas stood still for a long moment, staring at the empty landscape. Her hands clenched into fists.

"We bury him here," she said finally.

They didn't have shovels. They didn't have time. But they had their hands.

Wordlessly, they began gathering stones, piling them one by one over Smokey's body, forming a cairn. The process was slow, deliberate. Each rock placed was a weight upon their souls, a piece of grief, a piece of remembrance.

No one spoke, but the silence was heavy. It wasn't empty. It was filled with memories, regrets, and unspoken words.

Daryas lingered, her gaze locked onto the pile of stones. The others waited, giving her space.

Then, finally, she took a slow breath. "We keep moving."

The group turned, walking away from the grave. But as soon as they were out of sight, Daryas stopped.

"Go ahead," she murmured, her voice barely above a whisper.

No one questioned it. Cab gave a slow nod before leading the others forward, disappearing into the mist-like haze left by the purge. Miner didn't move.

Daryas stood there for a long moment, staring at the cairn. Her breathing was steady, controlled—until it wasn't.

Her shoulders trembled first. Then, slowly, she sank to her knees, pressing her gloved hands into the dirt.

A sharp, broken breath escaped her lips. Then another. Then the wall cracked.

A sob tore through her, raw and unrestrained. Her fingers curled into fists, nails digging into the ground as if she could somehow hold onto him, hold onto the moment just before it all went wrong.

She had always been a soldier first. Strong, composed, unshaken. But here? Here, there was no one left to fight. No orders to give. Only loss.

Her breaths hitched between silent cries, the kind that tore at the soul but made no sound. She clenched her jaw, trying to swallow it back, but it was useless. The weight was too much.

A scream built in her throat, and this time, she didn't stop it.

It ripped from her like a wound torn open, echoing through the emptiness.

Then, silence.

Cal stood frozen, watching as she crumpled in on herself, her body trembling with the force of her grief. It was raw, unguarded—something he had never seen from her before. Minutes passed, and still, she didn't move. The sobs faded, not into relief, but into something quieter, something emptier. She wasn't past it. She had just buried it. Like him.

Finally, she wiped at her face, took a deep breath, and stood.

Miner was still there, watching. He hadn't said a word, hadn't tried to comfort her.

She exhaled slowly, then nodded toward where the others had gone. "Let's go."

No more time to mourn.

The War Angels moved in silence, navigating the barren wasteland that had once been a stronghold. Miner adjusted the weight of his armor as they ascended a rocky incline, searching for a vantage point—somewhere they could raise communications and reach the stronghold.

The higher they climbed, the more the valley stretched out before them. But there was nothing. Just empty land, erased by the purge. A manufactured illusion of untouched wilderness.

When they reached the crest, Daryas exhaled. "This should work. Get the coms set up."

Cab and Grassie nodded, already moving to unpack what little equipment they had. Rich began scanning the horizon, keeping watch while the others settled in.

"Hey," Daryas looked at Miner. "You okay?"

Miner nodded. "I think so."

"Listen. The fact that you were...made, or whatever it was Varek said, that doesn't change anything. You know that right? You're still you."

He stared at the dirt for several long seconds. The air filled with the tension of the moment.

"Yeah," Miner said simply. There were implications there, meaning behind his origins that he didn't like. But now was not the time. He knew he could deal with that later. His mind flicked to his parents, wondering how much they really knew or suspected. He pushed the thought aside.

Daryas let out a slow breath, rolling her shoulders. "Before we make this vid call, we need to know exactly what we're doing. If we go in blind, we die."

Miner exhaled. "We go back, get into the stronghold, find Corvin, and take the data core. That part is clear. But what happens after?"

The group fell silent. The wind howled through the open space, kicking up dust over the smooth, untouched land left behind by the purge.

Cab finally spoke. "Even if we stop Corvin, we still have to deal with Varek. Even if we take them both down, the experiment doesn't stop. It just keeps going without them."

Grassie sat down, stretching out her legs. "So we don't just stop them. We stop the purge ships. Take them down and the experiment can't reset. That's what really kills this damned experiment."

Rich frowned. "We take out the ships, assuming that's even possible, you saw how big they are, and what then? We stay here? The experiment's done, but we're still stuck inside it. We need a way out."

Daryas ran a hand through her hair, thinking. "We can't take every stronghold. Not in any way that matters. We'd never win. So we need to make them purge their own system. Corvin called a purge on us once—he can do it again. If we force him, we can turn their own weapons against them."

"And if he refuses?" Miner asked.

"Then we make him," Daryas said simply.

Another silence settled between them before Cab finally sat down near the fire pit they had started building. "We figure out the details in the morning. Right now, we need to rest. We're no good to anyone dead on our feet."

One by one, the team took their places around the flickering fire, its warmth a small comfort against the cold reality they faced.

The silence stretched, the flames casting long shadows on their faces. It wasn't an empty silence—it was heavy, weighted with loss. Then, as if the tension had grown unbearable, Grassie let out a quiet chuckle.

"Smokey would've hated this."

Miner looked up. "What?"

She smirked slightly, shaking her head. "Sitting around, all serious. He would've been bitching about how depressing we are right now. Probably making some joke about how if we didn't start talking, he was gonna shoot someone just for fun."

Cab snorted. "Yeah. Remember that time he tricked a whole squad of rookies into believing he could smell the infected? Said he had 'the gift.'"

Rich actually chuckled. "And then he started randomly calling out 'they're close' just to mess with them. Had them on edge for hours."

Daryas gave a small shake of her head, exhaling through her nose. "Idiots nearly shot a harmless survivor because of him."

Miner listened, watching as the tension cracked just slightly, replaced by something else—something lighter. Then, as Grassie was about to say something else, she stopped, narrowing her eyes at Miner.

"Wait. You don't even know what we're talking about, do you?"

Miner hesitated. "I mean... I knew he was full of shit most of the time."

"No, no," Grassie said, sitting up. "You don't know what your armor can actually do. Do you?"

The fire crackled, the embers spitting into the air. Miner said nothing.

Daryas blinked, then slowly shook her head. "You've been wearing it, but you don't know what it can do."

"It's armor," Miner said, frowning. "It keeps me from dying."

Cab let out a sharp laugh. "Oh, you poor bastard."

Daryas stood up, brushing dust from her knees. "Alright. Get up. We're fixing this *right* now."

Before they could start, Cab gestured toward Miner's armor. "You can't go back in looking like that. Smokey bled out in that suit. It's still got the damage, the scorch marks, the blood. If we're doing this right, we need to clean it."

Miner looked down at himself. She was right. The blood—Smokey's blood—was still streaked across the chest plate, dried in places, smeared in others. He had been so focused on everything else, he hadn't even thought about it. The others hadn't said anything either, but they had noticed.

"We do it now," Rich said simply. "Before we get too used to seeing it that way."

They worked in silence, using rags, bits of cloth from their undersuits, and what little water they had left to wipe the armor down. It wasn't perfect—the deeper scratches and burns would still show—but the blood was gone.

It wasn't much, but it made him feel lighter. Cleaner. Like he wasn't carrying Smokey's death as visibly as before.

Daryas inspected him once they were done, nodding in approval. "Now, let's teach you how to use it."

Miner hesitated but followed as Daryas motioned for him to step away from the fire. She tapped his wrist console, and Miner's

HUD flickered to life, suddenly filled with data he hadn't accessed before.

"First thing's first," Daryas said. "Your mobility assist. That armor is designed for full sprinting speed, stabilization, and weight redistribution. You don't have to fight against it—you have to let it move with you."

Miner frowned, glancing at his boots. "How do I—"

Before he could finish, Daryas pressed something on his gauntlet, and suddenly—the weight on his body shifted. It wasn't gone, but it was... balanced. Like he wasn't wearing something nearly as heavy as it actually was.

"Whoa."

Daryas smirked. "Exactly."

Grassie stood, crossing her arms. "Targeting assist next. You ever wonder how Smokey always landed those impossible shots? It wasn't just skill, don't get me wrong, he was good even without the armor, but it takes you to the next level. The armor syncs with your weapon's sights and tracks movement faster than the human eye. It'll highlight threats before you even register them."

Miner looked at his rifle, then back at them. "And no one thought to tell me this sooner?"

"You didn't ask," Cab said, grinning. "And Smokey never would've told you. He would have thought it was funnier watching you struggle."

Daryas motioned for him to bring his rifle up. "Go on. Try it."

Miner raised his weapon, and his visor adjusted instantly, locking onto small heat signatures in the dark—rodents moving in the distance, dust shifts where the wind was breaking over the rocks. His aim settled, perfectly guided, faster than his own mind had been processing.

"Damn."

Daryas nodded. "Told you."

They went on, showing him the motion tracking system, the proximity sensors, the comms encryption—everything that made Vanguard armor more than just a suit. By the time they were finished, the fire had burned lower, but Miner felt... different.

More than just a soldier. More than just Cal.

"Now," Daryas said, settling back into her seat. "Tomorrow, we make the call."

The fire had burned low through the night, leaving only glowing embers and the faint scent of smoke clinging to the air. The wind had picked up, howling over the barren landscape, but it wasn't what woke them.

It was the weight of what came next.

Miner stirred first, blinking against the dim morning light. He felt heavier than before, but not from exhaustion. From something else—something deeper. A truth he hadn't fully processed yet.

The others woke in slow, silent movements. No one spoke at first. The usual quiet hum of pre-mission preparation was missing. There was no sharpening of knives, no idle chatter. Just silence.

Cab sat with her knees drawn up, staring into the remains of the fire. Grassie shifted, rubbing at her face like she was trying to scrub away the last remnants of sleep, or maybe the memories of what they had learned. Rich stood a little way off, his arms crossed, eyes fixed on the horizon.

Daryas was the last to sit up. Her expression was unreadable, but there was something different in the way she carried herself. Not just exhaustion. Not just grief. Something deeper.

Finally, Cab spoke. "It wasn't real."

Miner turned to her. "What?"

Cab's jaw clenched. "All of it. The war, the strongholds, the fighting. Our whole damn lives. None of it was real."

That statement settled over them like a weight too heavy to lift.

"We were test subjects," Grassie muttered. "That's all we ever were. Every mission, every deployment, every move we made—it was all scripted. They let us fight because they needed to see how we would."

Rich let out a slow breath, his voice quieter than usual. "I thought we were part of something bigger. I thought we were the ones protecting people. Instead, we were just... data points."

Daryas stared at the fire, her expression dark. "And now we have to fight the man we followed for years. The man we would have died for."

Silence.

Miner shifted uncomfortably. That was the part that stung the most. It wasn't just that they had been lied to. It was that they had followed without question. That they had trusted.

"I looked up to him," Cab admitted, shaking her head. "Varek. I thought he was everything a soldier should be. That he was protecting us. And now we know he's the one who made sure this all kept happening. He let us fight, let us die, knowing none of it mattered. And he still thinks he's doing the right thing."

"And Corvin?" Grassie scoffed. "That smug bastard doesn't even care. To him, this is just a puzzle. A damn equation he's trying to solve. And we're just variables."

Miner exhaled slowly. "So, what do we do with that?"

Daryas finally looked at him. "We make sure they don't get to keep doing this."

Rich nodded. "And we make sure they know we're not just test subjects anymore."

Miner glanced at the remains of the fire, at the ashes left behind. This was it. Everything they had known, everything they had believed in, was gone. Burned away. And now? The fate of all the people in the valley, of all the people in the entire set of valleys, was on them. They controlled the destiny.

Daryas moved towards the comms that Grassie and Cab had set up the night before.

"Get ready team. Miner, get that helmet on. They can't see you."

Miner nodded and pressed the helmet down over his head, feeling it snug itself into place. He nodded, assuming Smokey's usual, casual lean against the rocks in the background. Daryas pushed the button, and the screen came to life with two ominous words.

"Acquiring Signal"

Chapter 23 – The Razors Edge

The screen crackled with static before stabilizing, revealing Commander Varek's face. He was seated in his office, posture stiff, his sharp eyes scanning the image before him.

"Daryas," he said, voice steady but edged with something hard to read. "I have to admit, I didn't expect to hear from you."

Daryas kept her expression neutral. "We survived."

Varek leaned forward slightly, studying them. "So I see. Given the circumstances, that is... unexpected."

Miner kept his head down, his helmet locked in place. He couldn't risk even the smallest tell.

Corvin appeared in the background, stepping into view with his usual calm detachment. "Interesting. I was certain you had been wiped out. Yet here you are." His eyes flicked over them, analytical. "How?"

"We saw the ship coming," Daryas answered smoothly. "We had a feeling about what was going to happen. We ran. We didn't have a choice."

Corvin's gaze lingered. "And the miner?"

Daryas didn't hesitate. "We lost him."

Miner didn't move. Didn't breathe.

Varek exhaled through his nose. "That's a loss."

A loss. Just like that. No hesitation. No sadness. Just another soldier gone, another expendable piece erased.

Daryas kept her voice even. "We need an extraction."

Varek nodded once. "You'll be brought back immediately. Bandit's team is enroute. We have your signal."

The transmission ended.

For a long moment, no one moved. The only sound was the faint hum of static from the dead comm link.

Cab finally broke the silence. "Are we telling Bandit's team?"

Rich shook his head. "Too risky. The fewer people who know, the better."

Grassie exhaled slowly. "That means if this goes south... we might be fighting our own."

Silence settled over them, heavier than before.

Cab shook her head, rubbing a hand over her face. "We've spent our whole lives following orders, fighting beside these people. And now we might have to kill them? How the hell did it come to this?"

Rich's jaw tightened. "It was always like this. We just didn't see it. The moment we started asking questions, we stopped being soldiers."

Grassie let out a bitter laugh. "So we get to die as traitors instead? That's just perfect."

Daryas sat back, arms crossed, her expression unreadable. "We're not traitors. We're the only ones fighting for the truth."

Miner clenched his fists. "Doesn't change the fact that when this starts, it won't be Varek and Corvin pulling the trigger on us. It'll be people we fought beside. People who trust us."

Cab exhaled sharply. "Yeah. And we'll have to make a choice. Do we pull the trigger first, or do we let them?"

The question hung in the air, suffocating.

No one had an answer.

The flight back was silent. Miner kept his head down, sticking to Smokey's mannerisms, his posture. He let the helmet do the work. No one questioned it.

Bandit's voice crackled over comms. "You all saw it too, right? That wasn't just some random energy surge. What the hell kind of ship was that?"

Daryas glanced toward the others before responding. "We saw it. A massive light, like it was swallowing everything up. There was nothing left—not even bodies. It wiped the entire place clean."

A long pause followed. "That's not standard protocol," Bandit said finally, his voice quieter, more thoughtful. "That's something else. Something we weren't told about."

Varek's voice suddenly cut in over the channel, calm, controlled. "I'll look into it. What you saw will be handled on a need-to-know basis. Understood?"

Daryas nodded once. "Understood, sir."

The channel cut out.

Bandit took off his helmet and leaned in to speak to Daryas. He didn't want this on any comm channel. Miner, sitting right next to Daryas, just as Smokey would have been caught in the exchange.

"I don't like this Daryas. Too many unknowns. What the hell happened down there?"

Daryas stood studying Bandits' cold expression for several heartbeats.

"There's a lot happening. I can't talk about this now. But I've always been able to trust you, Bandit. I hope that holds true. For me and all of the War Angels. The Time Bandits have always had our backs. Just... just don't let that slip if the time comes."

Bandit studied Daryas for several seconds, glanced at Miner and put his helmet back on without saying a word.

Miner kept his head forward, his hands resting lightly on his knees, but inside, his heart pounded. They had played it off. For now, maybe even gotten an ally in Bandit. But Varek's interest was piqued, and Corvin's silence was even more unnerving. They weren't out of danger yet.

Bandit moved up front to talk to the pilots.

"Varek's watching us," Rich murmured to Daryas. "I can feel it. That wasn't just standard questioning. He's looking for something."

"Then we give him nothing," Daryas replied, her voice just as low. "Stick to the story. We saw a ship. We don't know what it was. We ran, and we survived. That's it."

Cab sighed. "Feels like we're balancing on a knife's edge. One wrong step and—"

"We don't get a wrong step," Miner muttered. "We make it back inside, we stick to the plan, and we don't give them a reason to look any closer."

They all nodded. Because if they slipped up now, it wasn't just their lives on the line.

They landed inside the stronghold, stepping onto solid ground that felt unstable. It was the same place they had left—but now it felt different.

The debriefing was tense. Varek watched them closely. His gaze swept over each of them, lingering just long enough to feel like a silent probe, testing for something unsaid. His eyes always came back to Miner.

"You survived an overrun stronghold, a full horde of infected, a mysterious ship with some kind of powerful weapon," Varek said slowly, his voice measured but laced with something beneath it—doubt, or maybe curiosity. "And you made it back here in one piece. I'd say that makes you either incredibly lucky... or incredibly resourceful."

Daryas nodded once. "We did what we had to. We weren't going to die out there."

Varek's fingers drummed against the table, his gaze narrowing slightly. "And you ran into no resistance on your way back? No Coalition survivors? No scavengers?"

Miner kept his posture rigid, his hands clasped behind his back, doing everything he could to channel Smokey's usual unbothered stance. He didn't speak. Didn't react.

Daryas answered smoothly. "The place was wiped clean. If anyone survived, they didn't stick around."

Varek hummed, leaning back. "Strange. No signs of life. No reports of scattered groups trying to regroup." His eyes flicked to Miner again. "And you, Smokey? You're awfully quiet."

The seconds stretched, suffocating in their weight. Miner felt his heartbeat hammering in his ears. If he spoke, would it give him away? He had spent enough time with Smokey to know his mannerisms, but could he replicate them well enough under this kind of scrutiny?

"Nothing to say about this whole ordeal? No remarks?" Varek stepped towards him, inviting him to engage in the conversation.

"He's still pissed about the whole thing," Rich interjected smoothly, giving an exaggerated shrug. "We all are. But you know Smokey. Hates talking about missions that go south. He's just glad to be alive."

Varek's eyes lingered for a moment longer, but then—he nodded.

Varek leaned back, studying them. "You'll return to your barracks. We'll talk more tomorrow. Get some rest."

They filed out of the room one by one, Miner trailing behind.

"Smokey" Varek called. The group paused, all of them trying not to appear tense. They had no choice, the other four continued to make their way out of the room and down the hall. Miner turned to look at Varek.

"Smokey, I don't like seeing you so quiet. Try not to let this get to you. Missions go south. People are lost. I know we all saw potential in him, but never forget that at his core: he was only a miner."

Miner stared, fury rising up that he could barely contain. The weight of his weaponry and the knowledge at what his armor could do to a man who was just standing there. So vulnerable. It was just the two of them, no one would be able to stop him from killing the man in front of him. They had a job to do, though.

Miner as Smokey, gave a curt nod, and turned to walk out of Commander Varek's war room.

Once inside their barracks, Miner pulled off his helmet, exhaling sharply. "That was close."

"What did he want?" Cab asked.

"Just wanted to make sure Smokey was okay. Took all my self-control not to shoot him between the eyes right there."

Rich's gaze flicked toward Miner, studying him for a moment before speaking. "You've changed."

Miner turned toward him, his expression unreadable. "We've all changed."

Rich shook his head. "Not like this. You're carrying something different now. It's not just anger—it's something sharper. You need to be careful. Bloodlust makes people reckless. And reckless people get killed."

Miner exhaled slowly, gripping the edge of the table. "I know."

Rich nodded once, his eyes steady. "Then don't forget it."

Daryas nodded, already pacing. "We don't have time to celebrate. That was the easy part. We need to move fast."

Miner reached into his belt pouch and pulled out the commander's access chip, pressing it into her hand. "Find the data core. Corvin is going to need it to initiate another purge. If we can stop him, we take control."

Daryas clenched the chip in her fist. "And you?"

"I'm going to Varek."

The room went still.

Cab frowned. "That's suicide."

Miner shook his head. "No. Varek wants me on his side. If I play this right, I can make him hesitate. Keep him occupied long enough for you to do what needs to be done. Plus, I have a plan that might turn this whole stronghold on its head."

Daryas exhaled. "You sure?"

Miner nodded. "We don't have another choice."

She pressed the access chip into her palm. "Then we move."

Miner made his way to the console in the corner. He had one piece of preparation to make. Hopefully, Varek still thought he was dead. If so, his access codes might still be active.

Miner made his way through the stronghold, his heart pounding against his ribs. The place was familiar, yet alien. He passed soldiers he had trained with, officers he had once obeyed. None of them knew. None of them suspected.

Then he saw him.

Joran, a haunted, sunken expression riddled his usually passive, mostly cheerful face.

Miner spotted Joran in the distance and made his decision instantly. He moved toward him, his steps measured, deliberate.

"Joran," he called, keeping his voice low but firm.

Joran turned, blinking in surprise, sunken expression turning to one of confusion and worry. "Me? What's going on?"

Miner didn't answer. "Come with me. Now."

Joran hesitated for only a moment before nodding, instinct overriding confusion. He fell into step beside Miner as they rounded a corner, moving toward an emptier part of the stronghold. The halls were quieter here, less foot traffic, less chance of being overheard.

Once they were alone, Miner stopped, turned, and reached up. He unlatched his helmet, the hiss of its latches releasing their seals filling the silence as he pulled it free.

Joran's breath caught. His eyes widened in shock. "Cal!?"

The name sounded foreign. Like it belonged to someone else.

Miner didn't correct him. Instead, he stepped closer, voice low. "Get people off the streets. Quietly. Things are about to go bad. Just make sure they're near an announcement monitor, though. That's crucial."

Joran hesitated, his eyes darting across Miner's armor, his expression shifting between confusion and suspicion. "Wait— Varek said you were dead. We all thought you were gone. What the hell is going on? Why a monitor?"

Miner exhaled sharply. "I don't have time to explain. Just listen to me. For all the years we've been friends, I just need you to trust me right now. You need to get people off the streets. Quietly. Things are about to go bad."

Joran's brow furrowed, his hand tightening slightly around the strap of his rifle. "Why are you in Vanguard armor? Did you—?" He stopped himself, shaking his head. "Did you kill one of them? How did you even survive?"

Miner stepped in closer, lowering his voice. "I told you, Joran. There's no time. I need you to trust me."

Joran searched his face, looking for something—an answer, a reason, anything to explain why the friend he thought was dead was suddenly standing in front of him, wearing armor that wasn't his.

Finally, his shoulders dropped slightly. "You always got into shit deeper than you should've, Cal." His voice was quieter now, but still holding that familiar edge. "I don't like this. But fine. I'll try."

Miner nodded. He didn't correct the name. Not this time.

Joran gave him one last look, then turned and disappeared into the alleyways of the stronghold, already moving to spread the word.

Miner exhaled, steadied himself, then turned toward Varek's command room.

Each step felt heavier than the last, the weight of Smokey's armor pressing into his shoulders. Not just physically—mentally, emotionally. Every inch of the stronghold he passed was a place he had walked before, but now he saw it differently. This wasn't home anymore. This was a battlefield.

The halls stretched on longer than they should have, or maybe it was just his mind playing tricks on him, drawing out the anticipation. The knowledge that Daryas and the others were somewhere behind him, working to carry out their end of the plan, did little to calm his nerves. Everything hinged on the next few moments. One misstep, one wrong word, and all of it would unravel.

Familiar faces passed by—they didn't stop him. Why would they? To them, he was Smokey, a Vanguard, one of their own. If only they knew.

The corridors blurred together, his boots echoing against the metal floor. The door to Varek's command room loomed ahead, its reinforced frame a barrier between Miner and whatever came next. He reached for the handle, inhaling sharply.

He stepped inside.

Varek turned, frowning. "What's going on? Smokey, can I help you with something?"

Bandit's hand dropped to his sidearm as Miner reached up to take off his helmet. Miner's eyes, now clear of the protective head piece, locked with Varek's.

Chapter 24 – The Cost of Betrayal

Varek's eyes narrowed as Miner set his helmet down on the desk between them, the heavy clunk echoing in the still air of the command room. Silence stretched for a long, agonizing moment.

Bandit didn't lower his weapon. His sidearm remained raised, aimed steadily at Miner's chest, his grip unwavering.

Miner could feel his pulse thrumming beneath his skin, but he didn't let it show. He had come this far. Now, it was about control—of the moment, of the conversation, and of Varek himself.

Varek exhaled through his nose, his expression unreadable. "I thought you were dead."

Miner tilted his head slightly. "You wrote me off pretty quick."

Varek's fingers drummed lightly against the desk. "It wasn't personal."

"It was to me," Miner said, voice even, though his hands curled into fists at his sides. "And to Smokey. He died saving me. You didn't even blink when Daryas told you I was gone."

Varek's lips pressed into a thin line. "A soldier dies, the mission continues. That's the reality of war. You, of all people, should understand that by now."

"War?" Miner let out a bitter laugh. "We both know this isn't a war. It's an experiment. And we're just the latest batch of test subjects."

Something flickered in Varek's gaze, a crack in the steel façade. Miner had him now.

Bandit's gun didn't waver, but his expression shifted—subtle, but there. He was listening.

Miner pressed forward. "How many times have you done this, Varek? How many Coalitions have you let burn, wiped off the map so the next set of survivors could take their place? How long have you played your part, moving us around like pieces on a board?"

Varek sighed, his fingers tightening into a fist against the desk before releasing. The weight of decades settled into his shoulders.

"It's bigger than you. Bigger than me," Varek said finally. "The system is all that matters. I was placed here to uphold it. To ensure it continues."

"And you never questioned it?" Miner challenged. "You never looked at the people dying under your orders and thought that maybe, just maybe, this was wrong?"

Varek's jaw tightened. His hands slammed down on the desk as he pushed himself to his feet. His voice exploded through the room.

"OF COURSE I QUESTIONED IT!" he roared, his voice echoing off the steel walls. Bandit tensed, but Varek didn't reach for a weapon. Instead, his hands curled into fists, his eyes burning with something deeper than anger. Resentment. Frustration. Regret.

His breath came hard and fast. "You think I started out like this? You think I walked into this job knowing the truth and just accepted it? I was just like you! I thought I could fix it. That I could stop it. That if I pushed hard enough, if I made the right choices, I could end the whole thing. Bring humanity back out into the world. I found out how! Did you know that? I found out how to leave this place. But when we learned that all of the expeditions turned up nothing, NOTHING, I realized our hope was here. We can rebuild the world, but not unless we have a united, controlled people."

He let out a bitter, humorless laugh, shaking his head. "But the more I fought, the more I saw the truth—humanity will always tear itself apart. I watched men turn on each other, watched Coalitions rise and fall, each one convinced they had the answer. Do you know what happened every time? Chaos. Factions. War. The same pattern. Over and over again."

Varek's fingers flexed at his sides. He wasn't just justifying himself—he was reliving it.

"The tests were the only way," he continued, quieter now, but no less intense. "Not because I wanted them to be, but because they had to be. You think the Coalition is the enemy? The virus? No. It's humanity itself. That's why this cycle can never stop. That's why we have to keep going until we get it right. Until we find the version of the world that doesn't fall apart."

He lifted his chin slightly, looking Miner dead in the eyes. "And you? You would destroy the best chance this place ever had at surviving. Without us guiding it? What do you think is left outside these walls? You think humanity will just... rebuild itself? It won't. It can't. The world is gone, Cal. And the only way we ensure that civilization doesn't collapse into chaos again is by refining this process until we get it right."

Miner's breath came slower now. "And how many times have you 'refined' it? How many resets? How many people erased from history because they didn't fit into your plan?"

Varek's voice was steel. "Enough."

A sharp beep sounded. An alert flashed across Varek's console.

His eyes flicked to it, and something in his expression shifted. Realization. Then, anger.

"What did you do?" Varek growled.

Miner straightened, keeping his voice calm. "You think this is just between us? That this is some private conversation? You've been broadcasting, Varek. Your entire command has been listening. Every officer. Every soldier. Every worker in this stronghold."

Bandit inhaled sharply. His gun wavered, just slightly.

Varek's expression darkened into something cold, dangerous. "You... you little—"

The room's comm systems flickered to life. Varek's own voice began replaying from moments earlier, a damning echo of his own words.

Miner let it sink in.

Then, with quiet finality, he said, "The truth's out, Commander. Now what?"

The moment stretched—a breath too long, a silence too deep.

Then Varek moved.

It happened in an instant. A blur of motion, a flicker of muscle memory honed over decades. His hand shot forward, gripping Bandit's pistol, twisting it in one fluid motion.

A shot rang out.

Bandit staggered back, a look of pure shock flashing across his face as a red bloom spread across the room behind his head. His weapon clattered to the floor, his body following half a second later.

Miner barely registered the sound. His instincts took over— he drew his sidearm and fired.

Varek was already moving, ducking toward the side exit. The bullets slammed into the wall behind him, sparks flying off metal.

"Bandit!" Miner dropped to his knees, but it was useless. The shot had been perfect. Quick. Clean.

Bandit was gone.

Miner clenched his jaw, his breath coming in short bursts. Not again. Not like this. The stronghold had been stripped clean by the purge, but now Varek was doing the same to his own people. The thought made his stomach churn.

He forced himself to move, grabbing his helmet and snapping it back into place. "Angels, report!"

Daryas' voice came through the comms, urgent, breathless. "We've got eyes on Corvin, but he's running. He's got the data core, but we're keeping him from using it by keeping him running."

"Keep on him," Miner ordered, his voice cold, controlled. He had to be. "Do not let him activate it."

A beat of silence, then: "Varek?"

Miner stood, his fists tightening. "Still breathing for now. He killed Bandit."

Daryas exhaled through the comms, then cursed. A painful, singular word that expressed the hurt and anger at the loss of another friend. Then a low, dangerous sound. "Then go get him. We'll handle Corvin."

Miner didn't hesitate. He pushed forward, charging through the same exit Varek had fled through.

The corridors were a blur of metal and shadow, his footsteps pounding against the floor. He had to catch him.

Then he rounded a corner—and stopped cold.

A line of guns raised.

Bandit's team stood between him and his target, their weapons trained on him.

Miner slowed, holstering his sidearm before lifting his hands, showing he wasn't reaching for his weapon. The hallway was too quiet, the only sound the faint hum of the facility's still-active systems. The smell of scorched air from Bandit's murder still lingered in his nose, mixing with the metallic tang of blood and sweat. He couldn't afford to make the wrong move.

"Varek ordered us to kill you," Jmeli said. Confusion laced her voice, but her grip on her weapon didn't waver.

Another stepped forward. "We all heard what he said. But then he told us it was a setup. That you were a plant. That you were working against the Coalition."

Miner felt his heart hammering in his chest. This was the moment.

One choice. One moment. One chance to turn them.

"Where's Bandit?" Nac asked. There was a sliver of doubt in his voice now.

Miner felt the weight of the truth settle over him. He met their eyes through his visor, his voice steady.

"Varek killed him."

Silence.

The weight of the next decision hung heavy in the air.

Then, a voice cut through the silence. A voice Miner had ever heard before and wasn't sure he ever would.

"Stop."

Fafa.

It was a single word, but it carried the weight of command, of something deeper than orders—conviction. The entire squad hesitated, their weapons wavering slightly as they turned toward him.

Sib stepped forward next, his expression hard. "Lower your weapons. We all heard what Varek said. And we all heard what he tried to cover up. Something isn't right."

The team exchanged glances, their fingers still resting on their triggers, but the doubt was growing.

Miner didn't waste the moment. "The War Angels need your help. We're fighting to stop this—to stop the purges, the experiments, the resets. We have one shot at this. If you stand with us, we can end this. If you don't, then I guess you better pull the trigger."

A tense second passed. Then Nac lowered his weapon. Jmeli followed. One by one, the barrels of their guns dipped toward the ground.

Fafa turned to Miner. "Go."

Miner gave a curt nod. "Get on this frequency." He rattled off the comms channel. "The Angels will need you. I'll handle Varek."

Without another word, he turned and ran, leaving them with their decision.

The hallways blurred as he sprinted forward. Bandit was gone. Varek had to answer for that, for everything.

The hallways twisted ahead of Miner like a maze, the distant echoes of alarms and hurried footsteps bouncing off steel walls. Varek was running.

Miner's breath was steady inside the helmet, but his blood burned with purpose. Bandit was dead. The War Angels were still fighting to keep Corvin from triggering the purge. And Varek was still alive.

That wouldn't last.

He took a sharp turn and burst into an open chamber—a private armory.

And standing in the center, sealing the last strap of a heavy, reinforced suit of Trexium-powered armor, was Varek.

Miner skidded to a halt. Varek had Vanguard armor.

The realization hit him like a blow. Cal had ever seen Varek fight, not really.. He had always commanded from behind the walls of the stronghold, never needing to prove himself in the field.

Varek flexed his hands, rolling his shoulders as the armor whirred to life, adjusting to his movements, it's red streaks catching in the light. His helmet rested on the nearby rack—he wasn't wearing it yet.

He turned, his eyes locking onto Miner. Cold. Calculated. No hesitation.

"You should've run when you had the chance. Apparently you're not as smart as we thought we made you," Varek said simply.

Miner pulled his rifle up, but Varek was already moving.

The first impact hit like a battering ram.

Varek crossed the distance in a blur, his fist slamming into Miner's chest, sending him staggering back into the wall. The armor absorbed most of it, but the force was still enough to rattle his ribs.

Miner barely had time to register the pain before Varek followed up, faster than he had any right to be. A knee to the gut, a forearm across the visor—

Miner twisted, bringing his gauntlet up just in time to deflect the next hit, driving his elbow into Varek's side. The strike barely fazed him.

This wasn't just brute strength. Varek knew how to fight.

Miner gritted his teeth. "Guess you like to get your hands dirty after all."

Varek smirked. "Someone has to clean up your mess."

They collided again, armor scraping against armor, the sounds of their struggle ringing through the chamber. Blows landed on both sides—neither gaining the upper hand, neither backing down.

Miner dodged a vicious hook, countering with a sharp palm strike to Varek's throat. Varek absorbed it, twisting into a brutal knee to Miner's ribs, the force enough to send a warning pulse through his armor's stabilizers.

The air was thick with the sound of their struggle—metal slamming into metal, the grating screech of armor locking against armor, the low hum of Trexium cores overworking to keep up with their rapid movements.

Then Varek seized him by the chest plate and hurled him backward.

The reinforced window shattered as Miner crashed through it, glass exploding outward as he tumbled down—falling, twisting—

Until he slammed into the courtyard below.

The impact knocked the breath from his lungs, his body skidding across the dirt as pain lanced through his shoulder. His HUD flickered wildly, recalibrating from the shock.

Everything stopped.

Soldiers, workers—the entire stronghold saw it.

Miner rolled onto his side, spitting blood onto the ground, his breath ragged inside his helmet.

A shadow passed overhead.

Varek leapt down after him, landing in a crouch. He rose slowly, his voice carrying across the stunned silence.

"I am the only thing standing between you and chaos," he said to everyone.

Miner pushed himself up, breathing hard. His visor was cracked, blood running down his face from where the impact had jarred him. His whole body ached, but he forced himself to his feet.

"No," he growled. "You're just another liar."

Varek lunged, aiming a devastating punch toward Miner's head. Miner barely dodged, sidestepping and delivering a quick uppercut to Varek's jaw, sending his head snapping back.

The crowd around them grew, soldiers watching, whispers spreading. No one intervened. Not yet.

Miner and Varek clashed again—brutal, unrelenting.

The fight was raw, an avalanche of blows traded back and forth. Every strike carried the weight of everything that had led them here—betrayal, sacrifice, vengeance. The air crackled with the hum of Trexium cores, armor servos whining with the force of their movements.

Varek landed a heavy blow to Miner's side, sending him stumbling. Miner retaliated with a sharp elbow, catching Varek across the jaw. The crack of impact echoed through the courtyard.

Then Varek's calm shattered.

He feinted left, then drove a boot into Miner's chest, sending him sprawling. Before Miner could recover, Varek was on him, slamming a gauntleted fist into his ribs. Again. And again.

"You're nothing, Cal! You were made in a lab. We'll just make another!" Varek snarled, kicking Miner onto his back. The breath was knocked from his lungs. His body screamed in protest, armor whining from the damage.

A second kick—then a third. Miner's vision blurred, pain roaring through him.

Varek loomed over him, lifting a weapon. This was it.

Then—

A trexium energy burst.

Varek staggered back, his armor sparking at the impact. It hadn't penetrated, but the force pushed him back and made him regain his composure. He whirled just in time to see Daryas, the War Angels, and the remaining Time Bandits walking toward them, rifles raised.

She didn't hesitate. Didn't waver.

"His name isn't Cal," she said, her voice sharp, unyielding.

She racked the slide, chambering another round.

"It's Miner."

She pulled the trigger.

Chapter 25 — Countdown to Oblivion

Miner lay in the dirt, his body screaming with pain, his breath coming in ragged gasps. His armor felt like it weighed a ton, pressing him into the cold ground. The world around him was a blur of movement and silence—stunned silence.

The crowd stood frozen, watching. Soldiers, officers, workers—all of them. They had witnessed Varek's downfall, saw the impossible unfold in front of their eyes. And now, they didn't know what to do.

Miner's ears rang, drowning out everything except the heavy pulse of his heartbeat. He forced himself to move.

A hand grabbed his arm, pulling him up. Daryas.

Another hand—Rich. Then Cab, then Grassie. The War Angels.

His legs buckled, but they caught him. Held him steady.

He swallowed past the blood in his mouth and rasped, "Corvin?"

Daryas' face was grim beneath her cracked visor. "Dead. We stopped him, but not before he activated the purge. The ship is already inbound."

Miner's stomach twisted. They were out of time.

The alarms blared above them—an eerie, mechanical wail that sent a fresh wave of panic through the onlookers. The stronghold was in chaos. Some soldiers were backing away, unsure. Others kept their hands near their weapons, waiting for orders that weren't coming.

Miner clenched his jaw and forced himself upright. The War Angels surrounded him, but beyond them was an entire stronghold teetering on the edge of collapse.

Then the first voice broke the silence. "What do we do?"

It came from one of the soldiers. A simple question, but it shattered the stillness like a bullet.

Then another voice. "Who's in charge now?"

Miner inhaled sharply. They were looking to him.

He couldn't afford to fall. Not now.

Other Vanguards stepped forward. They had just watched their commander die. Their world had been ripped apart, their beliefs shattered. But they were still soldiers. They still needed a leader.

And Miner—Miner was all they had.

"Help me get to the command center," he said, voice steadier than he felt.

A beat of hesitation, then they moved.

The Vanguards lifted him up, supporting his weight as they helped him forward. Not just the War Angels. All of them. The remaining Vanguard squads—fighters who had just watched their commander fall and were now looking to someone else.

To him.

They reached the command center, and Miner linked into the battle systems.

The interface flooded his HUD. Every weapon they had. Every soldier still standing. Every airship in the hangars.

Then, Daryas' voice cut through the comms, sharp and commanding. "Varek is dead." A beat of silence followed, then the weight of her next words landed. "Miner is in charge now. You listen to him, or you don't make it out of this."

A crackle of static, then a soldier's voice, skeptical and rough. "Who the hell is Miner?"

Daryas didn't hesitate. "The one who's gonna make sure you see tomorrow."

He didn't waste time. "This is Miner," his voice was steady despite the pain. "We need to bring that ship down before it reaches the stronghold. It will erase us from the map. All Vanguard units, prepare missile strikes. All pilots, load up. We're putting everything we have into this."

Commands were acknowledged. The Time Bandits—Jmeli, Sib, Fafa, and Nac—took to the skies, flying other Vanguards into position. Soldiers scrambled to prepare for what was coming.

Miner turned toward Daryas. "The data core. Give it to me."

She placed it in his hand. He inserted it into the system.

The access screen appeared. Locked.

Miner's heart sank. He couldn't override it.

He needed Corvin's personal access code.

Miner clenched his jaw, frustration spiking as his fingers hovered over the console. The screen blinked its cold refusal at him. No way in. No override.

"Damn it," he muttered under his breath. His mind raced. Think. Think.

Daryas leaned over, scanning the system readouts. "We don't have time for this. That ship is on its way right now. Who knows long we have."

Miner exhaled sharply. He could feel the weight of every eye in the command center pressing on him. Vanguards, officers, soldiers—waiting. Expecting.

"Okay, we pivot," he said, forcing control back into his voice. "When we see that ship we hit it with everything we've got. Every missile, every round, every—"

Miner paused as more dots appeared on his HUD. Then the tremors started.

A deep, rolling vibration carried through the dirt, subtle at first—almost like an aftershock from the earlier battle. But it didn't fade. It built, steady and deliberate, each pulse heavier than the last.

The floodlights swept across the ruins beyond the walls, their beams cutting through dust and smoke. At first, the movement in the distance could have been a trick of the light—a shifting haze, a ripple across the horizon.

The infected were coming.

The first row of bodies moved in uneven strides, some dragging limbs, others unnervingly steady. Behind them, more followed. And more. A slow, endless tide pressing forward, hundreds deep, swallowing the landscape in its march.

The radios crackled, voices overlapping. Someone swore.

Then the first screech cut through the air.

A shape broke from the clouds. Then another. And another. Flyers, dozens of them, their wings catching the floodlights in fleeting glimpses of exposed ribs and stretched, rotting flesh. They moved with purpose, weaving through the air, circling high before dipping into steep, sharp dives.

The radio flared again. "We have air threats—repeat, we have—"

Then came the impact.

A shockwave rolled through the stronghold as something massive stepped into view. A towering Grave Titan emerged from the haze, blotting out the distant fires with its immense form. The second followed close behind, each footfall dragging a fresh tremor through the ground. Smaller undead, breaking apart and reforming, swarmed around them, funneling into unnatural lines.

This wasn't a horde breaking through defenses. It was a force, moving with intent.

BEEP. BEEP.

Civilian markers flared green on Miner's HUD, dozens still scattered across the stronghold, unmoving. Too many still above ground.

He hit his comm. "All civilians, underground—*now!*" His voice carried across every active channel. "Mines are secure! Get down there and seal the gates!"

No one moved at first, stunned by the scale of the approaching nightmare. Then, finally, one worker ran. Then another. The dam broke, and the rest sprinted for the tunnels, tripping over debris in their panic to reach safety.

BEEP. One by one, the markers blinked off as they disappeared underground.

Miner exhaled sharply. Now it was just them.

The first shots rang out.

The front line of undead reached the barricades set up weeks ago by the build teams, and the moment they did, the stronghold erupted in gunfire.

The defensive turrets roared, spitting rounds into the mass of bodies. High-caliber rounds punched through rotting flesh, sending limbs and torsos spinning into the dirt. The first wave staggered, fell—then were clambered over by the ones behind them as the second waves pushed towards the stronghold defenses.

"All units, forward!" Daryas barked into Miner's comm link with the front lines.

The Flyers ignited their jetpacks, launching off the barricades in controlled bursts. They shot forward, weapons raised, engaging the first line of armored ground forces before they could breach the perimeter. Missile Vanguards took up position on the higher platforms, launching their payloads into the sky.

A guided missile screamed through the air.

It connected mid-flight, slamming into an undead flyer. The explosion scattered burning flesh, sending charred wings spiraling into the dark.

Another shriek. Another flyer dove low, talons outstretched.

A Missile Vanguard met it mid-air, colliding with its torso in a brutal tackle. They tumbled wildly through the stronghold, the Vanguard clutching its decayed throat as it twisted and screeched.

One clean shot.

A pistol fired point-blank, the bullet punching through its skull. The creature went limp. The Vanguard released, falling fast.

He hit the ground in a roll, absorbed the impact, and came up sprinting, rifle already rising.

Then the ground shuddered.

BOOM.

The first Grave Titan stepped into the light, massive, unrelenting. A second loomed behind it, the sheer weight of their movements shaking the battlefield.

The smaller undead moved around them, flowing like water, funneling toward the trenches in waves.

Then the purge ship, massive in size and scope, just like the one they had seen over the last stronghold, descended through the clouds.

Miner gritted his teeth.

"That thing is built for durability. Standard firepower won't bring it down fast enough," Rich's voice came from behind him.

Miner gritted his teeth, his mind racing. They had minutes. Maybe ten, if they were lucky. The purge ship loomed overhead, its spotlights sweeping over the battlefield, casting long shadows over the chaos below. The undead swarmed the trenches, their numbers seemingly endless, while the Grave Titans continued their relentless march forward.

The strongholds' forces were barely holding.

"We start with missiles," Miner said, forcing control back into his voice. "We time it right, we might be able to overload its defenses. It has to be powered by Trexium. Trexium cores can only handle so much incoming damage before they run out of power."

A Vanguard Flyer shot past the command center window, their jetpack blazing in the darkness as they tore into a squad of armored undead below, plasma rounds punching clean through rotting bodies.

Daryas nodded, barely looking up from the battlefield map. "We'll have to stagger our strikes. If we hit it all at once, it'll just absorb the impact and adjust. But if we keep the pressure constant—"

"It might force a vulnerability," Miner finished. "But that still doesn't solve how we actually take it down."

"We don't need to destroy it," Rich said. "We just need to cripple it. If we can take out propulsion, it won't make it over the stronghold."

A Missile Vanguard launched another guided strike from the rooftops. The missile locked onto a flyer, slamming into it midair, the explosion sending charred remains crashing into the battle below.

"That's assuming we can get past its defenses," Cab muttered. "We're throwing spears at a moving fortress."

A piercing shriek tore through the comms. One of the Vanguard Flyers went down, dragged from the air by a zombie flyer mid-dive. The two figures spiraled toward the rooftops— until a Missile Vanguard tackled the undead mid-air. They tumbled through the sky, a tangled blur of armor and claws.

A single gunshot.

The undead flyer went limp, its body twisting as it crashed through a lower barricade. The Vanguard rolled on impact, barely absorbing the fall before pushing back into a sprint. No hesitation. Straight back into the fight.

"All right," Miner said, voice sharp. "All long-range artillery, lock onto propulsion systems. Time Bandits—get our best shots into position. If we can ground it, we might just have a chance."

The comms crackled with acknowledgments. Below, the Grave Titans reached the first defensive wall.

BOOM.

One of them swung a massive, fused-metal limb, collapsing an entire section of barricades with a single hit. The undead poured through the gap, forcing soldiers to fall back to secondary lines.

The first missiles hit the purge ship.

The explosions bloomed against the hull, but it barely wavered. The shockwave rippled across its surface, but the ship pushed forward, undeterred.

"Direct hit—NO DAMAGE!" Jmeli's voice crackled over the comms, disbelief in her tone.

"Stay on it!" Miner barked. "Keep up the fire—don't let up!"

Miner turned to Daryas. "I need you out there."

Daryas and the rest of the War Angels nodded and, almost as if in planned unison, put their helmets on and filed out of the room. Before she left, Daryas turned to Miner.

"When the time comes, you won't be able to hesitate." She said, in a flat tone.

Miner nodded and turned his attention back to the command screens, his breathing difficult from what he presumed were broken ribs.

Daryas walked out the command door to join the battle.

More missiles launched. More air support engaged. Below, the ground war was turning desperate.

And the purge ship kept coming.

The ship had no counter-defenses, no turrets, no weapon systems—because it didn't need them.

"We're barely scratching it!" Sib called out.

Miner's stomach tightened. The Purge Ship remained steady, unshaken despite the relentless barrage of missiles and firepower. The Grave Titans were still moving. And the front lines were collapsing.

"Hold your fire on the ship!" Miner barked through the comms. "We need to deal with the Titans first!"

The first Titan reached the barricades.

BOOM.

Its fused-metal limb swung through a watchtower, splintering steel like rotted wood. A section of the defensive line collapsed, sending soldiers scrambling back toward the second line. Gunfire riddled the Titan's armored hide, but it barely reacted.

The first Grave Titan stepped into the firelight, a walking monolith of destruction.

BOOM.

A missile exploded against its shoulder, sending scorched flesh and metal plating flying—but the creature barely slowed.

"It's pushing through!" Cab shouted. "We need more firepower!"

Miner knew firepower wasn't the answer here. Rattling his brain he stepped to a window that overlooked the fighting below. He saw it.

The field was littered with wreckage—burning transports, ruptured fuel lines, scattered munitions from fallen convoys.

They couldn't break the Titan's armor—but they could use the debris and explosives already present on the battlefield.

"Daryas!" Miner's voice was sharp over the comms. "We need to *sink* it!"

"The hell does that mean?"

"We use the battlefield!" He sent a display of the wreckage strewn area to her visor. "That thing is heavy as hell. If we detonate the fuel lines of those vehicles and add in as many explosives as we can, we can blow a hole so big in the ground it'll fall in."

Daryas hesitated for only a second. Then she was already relaying orders. "Ground teams pile as many explosives as you can in its path! Missile teams! Adjust targets—hit the wreckage, not the Titan!"

The ground teams scrambled, their motion drawing the Grave Titan directly towards them. They scrambled to get away as quickly as they could before the first explosion ripped through the ground.

Flames burst outward, consuming broken vehicles and ruptured gas lines. The blaze jumped from wreck to wreck, igniting scattered ordnance in a deadly sequence of detonations.

The Grave Titan took another step forward—then its foot landed on unstable ground.

CRACK.

The ground caved.

The entire battlefield shifted as the ruptured terrain gave way. The Titan's massive weight was too much—it sank, the burning wreckage collapsing beneath it, shards of sharpened, broken metal slicing through hundreds of points on the body of the titan.

And then the final explosion hit.

The chain reaction reached buried trexium cells. The blast roared upward from beneath the Titan, an inferno of burning energy that tore through it from the inside out, leaving a crater behind.

The Titan bellowed, its body twisting as its armor shattered, its core structure rupturing from the blast.

Then, with one last violent tremor, it was gone—swallowed by the flames and the collapsing battlefield.

But the second was still coming.

"Arcus-One, we need a distraction!" Miner called through the comms, his plan continuing to take shape on the fly.

"We're in position. Tell us what you need."

"Get that titan under the ship. We're going to bring that ship down right on top of it." Miner said, steeling his resolve against the rising death tolls climbing up his screens.

The airship swooped lower, just enough to keep the Titan's focus.

The Grave Titan turned, drawn toward the movement.

Come on, you big bastard, Miner thought to himself.

The Purge Ship loomed above them.

"We need all fire on the Purge Ship now!" Miner called over the comms.

Every missile team, every artillery gun, every long-range weapon shifted focus.

The battlefield was overrun. The trenches had fallen. Soldiers were retreating in waves, fighting a losing battle against the endless tide of undead but Miner knew if they didn't stop the ship, nothing else would matter anyway.

"Target the underside!" Daryas ordered. "We don't know how it works, so we hit everything on my marked position."

The next wave of missiles launched.

The Purge Ship shuddered.

The first true damage bloomed across its hull. Dark energy surged from the impact zones, arcing across its exterior like veins rupturing.

"We've got an opening!" Grassie's voice cut in. "It's small, but it's there!"

"Time Bandits, get the War Angels inside!" Miner ordered.

"We're moving!" Sib's voice came back instantly.

Flyers peeled from their engagements, descending to pick up the War Angels. Engines roared as they lifted toward the breach point, adjusting their flight paths midair.

The comms buzzed with static and hurried voices as the War Angels entered the breach. Miner could hear Daryas' controlled breathing, the shuffle of boots against metal, the occasional creak of the ship's hollow frame.

"We're in," Daryas reported, her voice clipped. "Hull breach is tight. No resistance. No crew. It's... empty. This place is running itself."

A chill ran down Miner's spine. "That doesn't make sense. A ship this size can't function without a crew. Someone has to be running it."

"Not from the inside," Cab murmured. "This thing was apparently meant to be autonomous. Fully automated."

Outside, the battlefield was collapsing.

The second Grave Titan continued to stalk beneath the Purge Ship, still drawn toward the airship that had baited it.

But the stronghold forces weren't watching the sky anymore.

The moment the War Angels breached the hull, the firing stopped.

"All ground units—refocus on the battle!" Miner snapped through the comms.

"Roger that!" Jmeli's voice came back. "Adjusting fire!"

The remaining soldiers regrouped, their fire shifting back toward the trenches, where the undead had broken through. The line had all but collapsed, and the fight had devolved into brutal, close-quarters combat.

In the command center, Miner kept one eye on the War Angels' movement through the ship and one on the battlefield.

The stronghold was in chaos.

Arcus-One was still flying dangerously low, pulling the second Titan further away from the main fight. The massive undead lurched toward it, stepping over wreckage, ignoring the carnage around it.

In the trenches, soldiers fought with everything they had left.

The missile teams, no longer firing on the ship, launched payloads directly into the densest clusters of undead. Waves of bodies were shredded in the blasts, but they still kept coming.

"We're getting pushed back!" Cab's voice came over the comms. "We need air support!"

But there wasn't any left.

Miner knew it.

They had thrown everything they had at the Purge Ship. Now they had to survive long enough for the War Angels to finish the job.

Miner's eyes flicked to the battlefield interface. The pulsing red beacon of the purge ship loomed closer. The stronghold's outer buildings were already bathed in its shadow.

"Status on the core?" Miner asked, his fingers gripping the console.

"Not in sight yet," Cab chimed in. "Moving through corridors, but this place is a maze. We need time."

Time they didn't have.

Miner clenched his fists. Five minutes. That was all they had. He could feel it slipping through his fingers.

"You've got five minutes," he said, his voice steady, firm. "That's all I can give you."

"Understood," Daryas said. She didn't argue. She knew what was at stake.

Miner turned sharply to a nearby Vanguard. "Get me a crate of Trexium ore. Now."

The soldier hesitated for half a second, eyes flicking to the screen where the purge ship loomed closer. Then he nodded and ran.

Rich's voice crackled in the comms. "You're planning something, aren't you?"

"We can't just cripple it," Miner said. "We need to bring it down for good. And I'm willing to bet Trexium is the key to doing that."

"You want to destabilize Trexium inside the ship?" Cab's voice was incredulous. "That's not just crazy—that's suicide."

"Maybe," Miner admitted. "But we're out of options. Forget the core—you won't reach it in time. Get back to the breach. We're taking the Trexium as deep into the ship as we can before destabilizing it."

The Time Bandits swept in, hovering just outside the breach, their engines roaring as they carried a crate of raw Trexium ore beneath them. The metal container glowed faintly, the unstable material within pulsing like a living thing.

"Cargo incoming," Jmeli called over the comms. "Get ready."

The War Angels grabbed the crate as soon as it was in reach, dragging it inside. The moment their hands touched it, the weight threatened to drag them down, even with their armor's assisted strength. Every step forward was a battle against gravity itself. Each second dragged out longer than it should, the weight of the moment pressing down on them as much as the ore itself.

Four minutes.

They hauled it forward, deeper into the ship, past silent corridors and empty halls. Every footstep echoed ominously. The silence was worse than any battlefield.

"That's deep enough!" Daryas ordered. "Back to the breach. Now."

Three minutes.

Daryas stayed behind, pulling out the charges. She moved with precision, planting each one along the Trexium crate's casing. Her breathing was even, but Miner could hear the tension in it.

Every movement felt slower than it should. Miner could feel every heartbeat ticking down the seconds.

Two minutes.

The sky outside the breach was burning. Smoke trails from the battle filled the air, energy rounds tearing through the battlefield as ships maneuvered in desperate arcs. The stronghold itself trembled as the ship drew closer.

Daryas' hands moved methodically, setting the final charge. She exhaled, steadying herself. "Charges set!" she called. "One minute!"

Miner's voice cut through the comms like a blade. "Daryas, move!"

She hesitated, her hand hovering over the detonator. "I need to make sure—"

"It'll work! Get out of there!"

Thirty seconds.

Then the comms cut out.

The explosion detonated with an earth-shattering roar, the first shockwave blasting outward in a ripple of blue and white energy highlighted with pink veins of the unstable trexium. The ship groaned violently, its metallic frame twisting under the sheer force, Trexium-fed flames bursting from deep within its structure. Walls crumpled inward, collapsing like a dying beast as plumes of fire shot through the corridors, consuming everything in their path. The hull buckled, splitting open along deep fractures as the purge ship's once-imposing silhouette began to falter.

At the breach, Daryas fell.

"DARYAS IS DOWN!" Grassie shouted.

Miner's HUD locked onto her plummeting marker, tumbling fast toward the ground.

Jmeli's voice was sharp. "I've got eyes on her! Moving in!"

Miner's hands clenched into fists as he watched the display, his mind racing. Daryas' dot was falling too fast. Jmeli's was gaining—but not fast enough.

Ten seconds.

Above them, the ship detonated, splitting apart, its front half landing on the Grave Titan and sending it barreling to the ground as Arcus-One sped away towards the stronghold.

The shockwave tore through the air around everything, a seismic force rolling outward, shaking the very ground beneath them.

On Miner's the display, he saw Jmeli's marker, Daryas, the ground. He held his breath as he watched the three points of light converge.

Two Months Later

Chapter 26 – Over the Horizon

For the first time in anyone's memory, the stronghold hadn't moved. It remained standing, against all odds, its people-about half of what they had before the fight-still breathing, but now free.

The fear of the purge still loomed, an ever-present shadow over their survival. But the difference now was that they knew. They knew the purge ships could be destroyed. They knew that if the worst happened, the Trexium mines were their refuge as they had been for Miner and the Angels. Perhaps that was what was holding the experimenters back. They had seen almost none of the undead, and no response from what the people had begun calling 'The Architects'.

Miner thought it was a soft name, given the cruelty they had inflicted upon untold numbers of their test subjects. But that was going to come to an end.

He often still had his thoughts flicker back to that final battle.

The undead had surged, wave after wave, a relentless tide meant to break them. And for a time, it nearly had. The trenches fell, the stronghold walls buckled, and the streets ran thick with the dead.

But they had held.

The Vanguard had drawn the line at the final barricade, turning the stronghold's inner defenses into a killing ground. Bottlenecks funneled the horde into tightly packed corridors, where gunfire and explosives cut them down by the dozens. When bullets ran low, they used blades. When exhaustion set in, they fought anyway.

By dawn, the battlefield was silent.

Not because the horde had stopped—but because there was nothing left to send against them.

Miner stood on the overlook, the wind whipping dust and debris across the open plains beyond the stronghold. Below him, the wreckage of the purge ship sprawled across the excavation site like a massive corpse, its metal frame being stripped by workers, salvaging whatever they could use. This was different. Before, they had scurried from place to place, never staying long enough to build. Now they were staying. Now they were preparing.

"Not a bad sight," Grassie said, walking up beside him, hands tucked into her belt. "You ever think we'd get this far?"

Miner exhaled, glancing over at her. "Didn't think we'd be alive, let alone standing here making bunkers."

Grassie smirked. "Speaking of, Cab wanted you to check on the expansions in the mines. If the purge ever does come back, that's where we'll be running. And now we've got enough space for half the stronghold if we need it."

Miner nodded, his eyes trailing over the landscape. "Good. We can't be caught unprepared. Not again. Make sure they keep going too. We need room for us and whoever else joins us here. Our numbers look like they're going to start increasing soon."

"The people know it, too," Grassie added. "They're staying because they believe in this. Even with the risk. We're not just surviving anymore. We're building something. Something real and outside The Architects' control."

The midday sun hung high in the sky, casting long shadows over the stronghold's central square. The market had grown— more stalls, more traders, more life than Miner ever remembered seeing in one place for this long. The people were settling in, despite the risks.

A crowd had gathered near one of the larger assembly areas, murmuring among themselves. As Miner approached, heads turned, voices hushed. They were waiting for him.

A woman, older, her hair streaked with gray, stepped forward. Her expression was careful, her hands clasped in front of her. "We heard Varek that day. We've heard people talking," she said. "That we were nothing more than a test. That our lives were planned for us. That everything we thought we knew was a lie."

The woman hesitated before asking, "Are we safe now?"

Miner didn't answer immediately. The truth weighed too much to be spoken lightly.

Miner let his gaze move over the gathered faces. Men and women who had fought, who had run, who had lived in fear for their entire lives. He saw the unspoken question in their eyes— was it really over? Was the fight done?

He exhaled slowly. "Not yet," he admitted. "But we're safer than we've ever been."

The murmurs rippled through the crowd. Not the answer they had hoped for, but the one they needed.

"The Architects of this mad world know that we know," Miner continued. "They know that at least one stronghold, and soon others, have discovered the truth. That makes their experiment, their tests about how we'll react to a virus, how we'll change and adapt to fight it pointless."

He paused, thinking about this next words carefully. He had their full attention and more had joined since he started speaking.

Then another voice, hesitant but clear. "So, what do we do now?"

Miner turned his gaze toward the speaker—a younger man, barely past twenty, his hands wrapped around the strap of a scavenged rifle. There was no defiance in his voice, only uncertainty.

"Now we stay. We stay and fight. More strongholds will be moving into this valley any day now. More purge ships will come to clear out those who choose to stay with us, and we will be the ones to lead the charge, to bring them down and give people freedom. The Architects are scared. They haven't sent anything against us yet because they know that we can win, that we will win. Their armor is cracked. Together, we'll rip it open and escape from this artificial prison they've constructed. We'll find the outside world and make better for all of us."

"We've spent our whole lives running," an older man spoke next, his voice rough from years of dust and hardship. "Every few months, we packed up and moved because Varek told us to. We fought because we had to. We survived because there was no other choice. But now... we have a choice."

Miner took another step forward, letting his gaze sweep over the crowd. "For the first time, we're not just surviving. We're building. We're thinking past the next month, past the next move. But the truth is, we don't have all the answers yet. What we do have is a chance. We have people who are listening, who are questioning everything they've been told. And that's how it starts. Not with a single fight, but with people willing to stand their ground."

The woman who had spoken earlier lifted her chin. "And if they come for us again? If they send more purge ships?"

Miner met her gaze. "Then we do what we did last time. And we make sure they regret it."

A ripple of agreement passed through the crowd, some nodding, others muttering amongst themselves. The nervous energy shifted into something else—something stronger.

"And the other strongholds?" another voice called. "Are they with us, or will we be fighting them, too?"

The steady rhythm of boots against stone echoed behind him, distinct, measured. Miner didn't need to turn—he knew that step.

She emerged from the edges of the crowd, the sunlight catching against the faint scars that now lined her face. The War Angels had seen her, but the people—the civilians, the ones who had whispered about her fate—had not. A ripple moved through them as they realized she was alive.

She didn't hesitate, didn't let the weight of their stares slow her down. She walked straight to Miner's side, data pad in hand, as if the past months had been nothing more than another mission.

"We've made contact with three strongholds so far," Daryas said, her voice calm, controlled, but carrying that edge of command only she could wield. "Some of them are listening. Some of them aren't ready to hear the truth yet. But we keep working at it. We keep spreading the truth, and when the time comes, they'll have to make a choice—just like we did."

The murmurs in the crowd shifted from shock to something steadier—certainty. Seeing the leader of the War Angels, even scarred, battered, and bruised, brought new life to the people.

Miner nodded. "This isn't over. But for the first time, we're in control of what comes next. And that's more than we've ever had before."

The crowd murmured, conversations breaking out in small pockets, but there was no more fear in their voices.

No one knew what was coming next. No one had all the answers. But for the first time, they weren't waiting to be told what to do. "We're not moving anymore. Not running," he continued. "For the first time, we've held our ground, and we're still standing. We know the truth now. That's something no other stronghold has had before us. We have a chance to change things. To stop the whoever it is that controls all of this. But it won't be easy. It won't be quick."

From the back of the crowd, someone called out, "What happens next?"

Miner took a long breath, then spoke. "We build. We fight. We win."

And for the first time, he saw it.

Hope.

No one knew what was coming next. No one had all the answers. But for the first time, they weren't waiting to be told what to do.

The crowd started to break up, individuals stepping up to shake his hand, thank him. Get a kind word from Daryas or any of the other member of the War Angels. They had become legends, icons to the people here.

Miner walked to the outskirts of the stronghold, looking out over the horizon. The wreckage of the purge ship still smoldered in places, a reminder of what had almost been their end.

The War Angels joined him, one by one, stepping onto the overlook. Daryas was the last, standing beside him, her arms crossed, her gaze locked onto the horizon. Rich leaned against a support beam, arms folded, silent but watchful. Cab and Grassie sat on a nearby crate, their postures relaxed but their eyes carrying the weight of everything they'd endured.

"So this is what winning feels like," Grassie muttered.

"Feels weird," Cab admitted, rubbing the back of her neck. "Like we're waiting for the other shoe to drop."

"It probably will," Rich said. "They're not just going to let us go. They'll come for us, eventually."

Miner nodded. "Soon, the strongholds that are supposed to take our place will show up. That will be the big challenge. We know everyone here. They're all new. No reason to trust us. And I'm sure whoever runs this is probably going to try and stop us."

Daryas exhaled, shaking her head. "Let them. We'll be ready."

Miner remained silent for a long moment, letting the conversation settle. Finally, he spoke. "You think they'll really come for us?"

Daryas glanced at him. "I'd be disappointed if they didn't. We did take down a purge ship after all."

Grassie huffed a small laugh, shaking her head. "Always looking for the next fight."

"No," Daryas said, looking back toward the stronghold. "Just wishing this would be the last one."

The others nodded, understanding unspoken between them. For the first time in their lives, they weren't just waiting to survive. They were waiting for a future they could build—together.

Epilogue

The convoy emerged over the horizon, its silhouette stark against the morning sun. Another stronghold. Another cycle.

But this time, it wasn't Miner's people on the move.

Miner stood atop the watchtower, his arms resting on the railing, watching as the new arrivals descended into the valley. The convoy was well-armed, organized, its formation tight. They moved like every other stronghold before them—because that's what they were. The next in line. The ones meant to take their place.

Only Miner's stronghold had never left.

Daryas stepped up beside him, eyes narrowed. "That's them."

Miner nodded. "Right on schedule."

She exhaled, watching the way the Vanguard patrolled the edges of the convoy, scanning for threats. "They're expecting to find an empty valley."

"They're expecting a lot of things," Miner replied humorously. He straightened. "Send out the scouts. Set a meeting."

Within minutes, the signal was sent, and the response came back quickly—cautious, but not hostile. They wanted answers. So did Miner.

The meeting was set on neutral ground between the two strongholds

Miner, Daryas, and the War Angels walked out first, moving with purpose. They stopped at the center of the open terrain, waiting. The new stronghold's commander arrived moments later, flanked by his advisor and a small escort of soldiers.

Their expressions were a mix of caution and confusion.

For a long moment, neither side spoke.

Daryas was the first to step forward. "We need to talk."

The commander tilted his head slightly, watching her.

"Your Vanguard," she continued. "Can we speak? One-on-one. No weapons, no orders, just a conversation."

The commander exchanged a glance with his advisor before asking. "Why?"

Daryas attempted to smile disarmingly. "Consider it a warrior's prerogative." She nodded toward the War Angels. "We'll take them off your hands for a while. Let them see what we've built here. They, and you, might find it useful."

The commander hesitated, his grip tightening slightly at his side. Then, finally, he gave a short nod. "Fine. But I want them back in one piece."

Daryas chuckled, motioning for the War Angels to follow her. "That depends on how much they argue."

With that, she and the War Angels moved toward the convoy's waiting Vanguard, leading them away toward the stronghold.

Miner and the commander stood across from each other, the air between them filled with unspoken tension.

The other commander's gaze swept over the stronghold in the distance before settling on Miner. "This place wasn't supposed to be here."

"No," Miner agreed. "It wasn't."

He reached into his coat and pulled out the data chip. The commander's eyes flicked to it, his expression immediately shifting.

Miner held it up between his fingers. "You recognize this, don't you?"

The commander exhaled sharply, then reached into his own belt. He pulled out an identical chip.

Miner nodded slightly. "Then we both know what that means."

The commander turned the chip in his hand, studying it. He was testing the moment, seeing how far Miner would push it.

"Miner," he said simply, tucking the chip away. "That's my name."

The commander regarded him for a moment longer, then finally returned his own chip to his coat. "Rogan."

They had their introductions. For the first time since they had arrived, the tension between them eased just slightly.

Rogan let out a short breath, glancing back toward his convoy. "So," he said. "Why are you still here?"

Miner's expression didn't shift. "Something went wrong."

Rogan's brow furrowed slightly. "Wrong how?"

Before Miner answered, he tilted his head slightly, his voice calm but firm.

"I need to know first," he said. "Who else knows?"

Rogan stilled. The question was obvious—if you knew. The advisor exchanged a brief, hesitant glance with him. It was small, barely a flicker of a reaction. But it was enough.

Rogan turned back to Miner. His voice was quieter now. "Just us."

Miner nodded once, letting the confirmation settle between them. That was the answer he needed.

"Good," said Miner as he exhaled slowly, shifting his stance. "That simplifies things."